Charles Franklin Thwing, Carrie Frances Butler Thwing

Carrie F. Butler Thwing

An Appreciation by Friends

Charles Franklin Thwing, Carrie Frances Butler Thwing

Carrie F. Butler Thwing
An Appreciation by Friends

ISBN/EAN: 9783337062590

Printed in Europe, USA, Canada, Australia, Japan

Cover: Foto ©Raphael Reischuk / pixelio.de

More available books at **www.hansebooks.com**

Carrie F. Butler Thwing

AN APPRECIATION BY FRIENDS

TOGETHER WITH EXTRACTS
FROM HER

"JOURNAL OF A TOUR IN EUROPE"

CLEVELAND, O.
THE HELMAN-TAYLOR COMPANY
1899

Contents.

Introduction.

TO the interpretations of the life and character of Carrie F. Butler Thwing, which gracious friends have made, it is fitting that certain statements of matters of fact be added.

Carrie Frances Butler was born in Farmington, Maine, 30 April, 1855. Her father, Francis Gould Butler, was, as is said of him in a sketch written by his daughter, a "quiet, country gentleman." He was possessed of large abilities of many kinds. He was primarily a banker, but he was also a great citizen. During a life of eighty years he was the most conspicuous man of his town and of that part of the State in which he resided. Her mother, Julia Wendell, is in the sixth generation directly descended from Evart Jansen Wendell, the immigrant ancestor of a family, long distinguished in American life and letters. A woman of great vigor of mind and body, she has throughout a long life given,—and is still giving,—herself, with great enthusiasm, to the concerns of her home, her church, and her community. To Mr.

and Mrs. Butler were born four daughters, of whom one, and she the youngest, alone lived to reach mature years.

Among the chief facts of this life, besides those referred to in the following pages, are: the preparation for college in the Wendell Institute, under the charge of Julia H. May and Sarah R. May ; the entrance into Vassar College at the beginning of the academic year of 1872; the retirement from Vassar College, because of ill health, near the middle of the Junior year ; and the taking up of residence in Cambridge, in the fall of 1879, having at that time married Charles F. Thwing. She lived in Cambridge until 1886. For the four years following 1886, her home was in Minneapolis; and in the fall of 1890 she removed to Cleveland, where on the 24th of April, 1898, she died. To her were born three children, one in Cambridge and two in Cleveland.

Of the journal which forms the larger part of this volume, it should be said that it was written in the course of the journey which it describes. At the close of a day or of a period, Mrs. Thwing recorded the impressions of the interval which it covers. She had no thought, at the time of writing, of printing what she wrote. The writing was done simply for the purpose of fixing impressions. The record is now printed by me chiefly for the reason that it embodies the qualities of her mind and heart in a better way than almost anything else that she has written. It is printed as she wrote it, with the exception of certain omissions of a personal character. I may add that I have thought of printing also certain of her letters together with some extracts from articles of her writing, but I shall not, at least at present.

In a letter written to his brother Carl, soon after the death of his wife, under date of 12th January, 1778, Lessing says, "they say it is only praise of one's self to praise one's wife." To those who knew Mrs. Thwing it is as needless, as it would be unfitting, for me to praise her. Should the book fall into the hands of those who did not know her, I can only say, as Lessing wrote to his brother Carl also of his own wife, "but if you had only known her."   C. F. T.

24 April, 1899.

The Years in Farmington.

THE church seemed very large and all the faces new and strange the Sabbath that I joined the "girls' class" at the Old South. The kindly pastor (Mr. Howard), and superintendent (Mr. Merrill), knew where the strange child would find a welcome. From the moment in which I was made to share the lesson, reading the texts from Carrie's Bible, I was possessed with the home feeling in regard to that church and Sunday-school which has always remained. Her dignity and grace were so combined, even at that early age, that I became a willing captive to the charms whose fetters tightened with the passing years. And it may not be surprising that after thirty years I can readily recollect to the veriest trifle the garments she wore that day.

Somewhat later our new pastor, Mr. Marden, formed a class for the study of "Pilgrim's Progress." Here we found help in Carrie's "marked references" in the same little Bible, and had the kindly loan of helps upon the subject to be discussed, from her home library.

Still later, at the time of her conversion, how precious that Bible became to her; and I learned to love my own the better for the new light that had fallen from hers.

———

The grave old doctor placed his foot upon his trunk and poised a vial upon his thumb and finger. I knew the gestures so well that I hastened to turn my face before he pronounced "No more school this term!" But instead of tears, the happy surprise of a smile.

A thrifty, saucy, and brilliant geranium bloomed upon my window-sill. Learning that the same fever had stricken me from which she was seriously ill, Carrie had forgotten her own woes in order to relieve mine. Words can never express the eloquence of that sermon! Flowers far more rare and costly often fail to reach my heart, but a gleam of the single scarlet geranium still stirs my pulses. And when we went from the "May School," it was out of love for her and that kindly deed that I wore "the single scarlet geranium" upon my graduation dress.

———

The winter day was drawing to its close when the door of an invalid's room opened to admit a huge express package. The contents proved to be the softest, warmest and handsomest California blanket obtainable. A complimentary note from Carrie explained that when she received the gift of a pair of blankets she could not refrain from dividing their warmth and beauty with her friend.

————

The evening before my visit to a large city was passed with Carrie.   We talked of the churches I should visit, the excursions to places of historical interest, and the libraries and art galleries to be seen.   As we said good-bye she placed a sealed letter in my hand, ''not to be opened until you are home-sick.''   What school-girl, visiting a Canadian city for the first time, failed of home-sickness?   And the seal was broken to find a crisp American greenback of generous size, to be taken at once to the money-changers; and before the money was spent I had learned many lessons through her generosity.

When we consider that these acts were performed by a child, spontaneously and without suggestion from others, is it a wonder that many have been blessed in her ?

My pen gladly presses forward to the Christmas day when it was my privilege to introduce to her my life-long friend and her future husband.   I remember, too, another day, ten years later, when, for an hour, she and I left our little children and sat again under the trees on the river bank.

FLORENCE GOODRICH–VARNEY.

The Years in Vassar College.

WOMEN'S education in the United States twenty-five years ago was far less a matter of course than it is today. There was a flavor of adventure about it that was absorbing, if not final. Hardly any group of women gathered in the few institutions claiming the title of higher, without some at least who felt high purpose and keen, if vague, ambition. There was a pulse of expectancy in the air of dormitories and of class-rooms. The present stretched alluringly far and wide, full of suggestion, infinite with possibilities. The result was that most of us felt ourselves to be as vaguely powerful as our surroundings were indefinitely stimulating. In the routine of our deeply significant, though somewhat submerged lives, our sense of imperfection and inefficiency took on the aspect of everlasting tentative. We had all the consolation of eternal youth in our absorption in what we were doing. The reflection from the wide outlook of our teachers attached to our view of ourselves and, atoms as we found ourselves in the impersonal life about us, we secured compensation in the sense of identity and of share in all stages of that life. So most of us felt more courage and took greater risks than we would have shown at home. The corporate life embraced and supported us in so many ways that it was no wonder that we thought it endless, nor that, as parts of it, we fancied ourselves serene and imperturbable. Our teachers and our friends sometimes wondered at this daring. They were seldom without surprise at the difference between the quiet, uninsistent girl before she went to college and the apparently reckless member of one of the four classes.

To this day I remember the feeling of buoyant, almost insolent, well-being that used to pervade the crowds in the Vassar halls. I shall never forget how after one had got thoroughly into the atmosphere, misfortune, calamity, death itself and carking anxiety seemed to withdraw. Later notice of them seemed intrusive, spiritually impertinent, properly relegated to the short vacations, or to the end of the college year. Even the friendly services owed and rendered to our friends lost force and poignancy by repetition and by becoming part of a system so big that fear was swallowed up in organization and in inefficiency. For four years the ordinary college student of those early days was one of the immortals. Theory and experiment supplied the touch of the infinite that is the hopeful side of the unfinished and the incomplete. We were lost in a maze of propitious conjecture and found ourselves in every prosperous happening about us. I do not know that we expected anything definite of ourselves or of our way of living. We were still too young for that, but we did feel that all time was ours and that it was ours for the same inconclusive uses that we were making of it then. We were perfectly familiar with the proverbial philosophy about mortal man and fleeting time, but for us time stayed and the mortal put on immortality. Duty lost much of its imperative and took on privilege and wide spaciousness for easy endeavor. The costly and careful system about us seemed made that we might work out the profitable experiments we felt ourselves to be. Even physical health ceased to be a problem; we took it as it came with a serene interest in complications as aspects of variety, at once pleasing and remunerative. We had the confident appetite for life resulting from the preparation and self-denial which had brought us to college and had kept us in ignorance of what our freedom and immunity cost. We were all hungry for experience, and most of us were quite ignorant of what it meant. We assented to propositions about sorrow and the lot of man, but we felt that sorrow was interesting and, in a high sense, ornamental. Ulysses, the much-enduring, was a hero with strong claims on our sympathy; and strength was synonymous with 'efficiency.

So our life went on in symbol for some of us, in dumb show for others, but there was everywhere a sense of more being intended than was expressed, I am sure. I, for one, felt that we were living in a character writ small against possibilities practically infinite. On the chance of entertaining angels unawares, it was well to be patient with folly and eccentricity. In the vast reaches of human development, present disagreeableness never seemed material for crises. Doubtless there were persons of our age who felt small anxieties, possibly suffered from narrow incomes, or from excessive diffidence, but we were easy about them after all on the ground that they would see the error of their ways and come to rest in the strong sweep of the ideal life as it moved forward. Then there were some ungracious beings who fumed and fretted about the misfits of human life, others who, clothed in the little brief authority of their learning, moral superiority or social position, strutted offensively and made ugly caricature of themselves in their callowness, but we felt that they would work in finally, and meantime they added to the complexity of the scene before us.

In this temper of ours, the history brought to us down the tide of the years was no less ours than that spread out day by day on the reading room tables, and ours no less than the contributions doled out to us at the end of the corridor by the teacher who stood guard over the legal trust represented by every batch of United States mail. By degrees we came to feel ourselves indestructible. Privileged with an all-embracing privilege. At least this was the experience of many who, like myself, were keenly sensitive to the influence of the corporate life about us. The emphasis on the communal personality seemed to extend our boundaries and make us all vital at every point of contact with the past or the present, the ideal or the real.

My experience had been increasingly of this sort when one day I heard a new voice in the recitation room. It did not have the assertive ring with which I was so familiar that I no longer listened to it. The speaker was a slender, pliant-figured girl, and what she said cut curiously across our ordinary class-room utterance. It was intensely suggestive, almost alien. One of my neighbors touched my elbow and whispered, "She's been reading Emerson; she's from Maine." In the light of this information I tried to account for the impression of aloofness that I had gained, but to no avail. Neither reading Emerson nor coming from Maine would explain this curious mixture of pathos and insight and conclusiveness. One of her classmates said of her, "Isn't Carrie awfully mature? I wonder if all the people where she lives were born furnished with ready-made Emerson?" I listened with interest, for it did not

seem to me that the most notable feature of what I used
to hear from Carrie was its resemblance to Emerson's
essays. Her manner showed a like individuality. There
was a subtle difference between her chance joining in the
group of girls energetically discussing some matters
beyond the fire-wall in the corridor, and that of the other
students. Her smile, slight, delicate, and somehow suggestive of gentle indulgence, was ready, but fleeting.
She carried with her always the air of one whose interests
were radical and self-supporting. I used to notice that
we always seemed to have been an episode in a much
more comprehensive experience she was having before
we appeared. To this she returned with satisfaction,
but without ardor, when we called for no further attention. Most of us, I think, never got within the inclosure
of her deepest experience, and few of us felt any certainty
that we had ever really come into her serious interest at
all. It was soon rumored that Carrie was disappointed
in the college, that she found too many of us lesson-
learners, instead of students, that she supposed we would
care less about what our teachers thought of our recitations and marked them for, and more of what we could
get out of study. There were discussions about the justice
of this characterization of Carrie's, but we finally decided
that our temper was natural, our way of living spon-
taneous, and likely to last. We heard, too, that Carrie

was very delicate and obliged to husband her strength much more carefully than the rest of us did. We reflected on our nightly luncheons of potted ham and lady-cake, our neglect of the dinner hour when the view from Richmond Hill proved more than ordinarily attractive, our satisfaction in wasting good hours of carefully scheduled time to make up for them by breathless minutes of exhausting concentration of mind on our work, and into the midst of our satisfaction at our own coarser endurance crept a feeling of awe of Carrie. What was the law of the world where she dwelt apart? What were its rewards? Her companionships were after the same remote sort. The common ground was not that of conviction, nor of cheap enthusiasm, but of the fine essence of character. Yet it was not a thin, poor, nor gossamer substance. For her insight was not concerned with mere spectacle. Under the shows of things she sought for the soul and for the permanent principle. She had a fine scorn for the petty, the shifty, and the devious. The innocent mummery in some of our social forms had no spell to bind her glancing fancy or her practical sagacity. It was clear to the least observant of us that she drew from other sources of supply than ours, and judged by other standards, and was impressed by other values.

But we had hardly suspected all this and begun to concern ourselves with what it might portend when we learned part of Carrie's story—only in time to realize dimly what it must have meant to her that her daily life was lived in the very shadow of death. Small wonder that she had larger store of the ideal than we. Her appeal to the absolute was in the nature of things more direct than ours, her relation to it more intimate. We dared question whether her limpid, attentive glance had gained any of its gentle, humorous persistence from looking death in the face, and from bearing with pain. Was her generous scorn the revolt of a strong spirit? We began to see how her difference from us had arisen. Her freedom in bonds was a spiritual criticism on our cheery delusion of the incomplete as the infinite. What her relation to us was, some of us, and those, perhaps, who owed her most, could never know. Spiritually, she dwelt apart, and when one day we learned that she had left college, we wondered whether we had helped or hindered, jarred or helped to harmony the fine-drawn chords of that experience so exceptional in the midst of our strenuous self-expansion. We did not forget her. She had made herself a part of our history at its very sources, and we always felt that in losing her we had lost possibilities of indefinite and always interesting importance. Sometimes, with a reminiscent smile at our crudeness and callowness, we have wondered whether a gracious blindness withheld her keenest inquiry, or whether the urgent claims of her short, full life already asserted themselves.

MARY AUGUSTA JORDAN.

The Years in Cambridge.

THE fall of 1879 will always be full of pleasant memories to those who then formed the parish of the North Avenue Congregational Church of Cambridge. They had called as their pastor the Rev. Charles F. Thwing, and his acceptance of the call had given the most complete satisfaction.

The ordination and installation services took place on September 25th, 1879, and a short time before that event, the young minister was united in marriage to Miss Carrie Frances Butler, a native of the same town as himself. It was an ideal union based upon the true love that only congenial souls can feel. She was especially fitted for the position she was to occupy, not only by intellectual abilities which were of the highest order, but also by the Christian graces that always adorn a consecrated life.

Not wishing at once to assume the cares of housekeeping, Mr. and Mrs. Thwing engaged board in the parish. Three homes in the parish successively opened their doors to receive them. In one of them, in October, 1880, their eldest daughter, Mary, was born. In the first year of her babyhood they removed to their third home. After spending a few happy months there, they began housekeeping in a house on Arlington Street, Cambridge, purchased for them by the father of Mrs. Thwing. There they formed what was ever known among the parish as an ideal home.

Mrs. Thwing entered with enthusiasm into all the plans of the new pastor for work among his people. With simple dignity and a gracious word for all, she soon gained a warm place in their hearts. This love of the people was fully reciprocated by her, and she loved to visit them in their homes, especially when in sickness or trouble. These tender relations continued throughout the seven beautiful years of her Cambridge life.

She was greatly interested in the temperance reform and joined the Cambridge Union soon after making her home in that city. In September, 1880, she became its President, and proved herself such an efficient officer, that, as one of its members expressed it, her coming among them was indeed a "Godsend."

In March, 1882, she made an eloquent plea before the Board of Aldermen at the City Hall, against granting license for the sale of intoxicating liquors in any part of Cambridge, especially in Ward Five, where she resided. Such was her interest in temperance instruction for children, that in compliance with the request of the Superintendent of Public Schools, she addressed the teachers upon that subject, in the City Hall, on the afternoon of February 25th, 1884. Other addresses followed, which were favorably received. At their close the Superintendent said that hereafter teachers would be required to give the instruction so urgently called for.

The W. C. T. U. were permitted to furnish the books required, and the Cambridge Union, of which Mrs. Thwing was president, had the pleasure of furnishing the books for Wards One and Five.

This cordial endorsement of her work was a great encouragement to her. Her modest self-possession well fitted her to speak in public, and she was never at a loss to express herself clearly upon any subject.

In company with a lady of the parish who was ever ready to assist her in any good work, Mrs. Thwing distributed votes at the Cambridge polls in the interest of temperance. Surely in this cause, so dear to her heart, she was indeed a blessing to the city of which she grew so fond as the years went on.

She soon found plenty of work in the parish which she was only kept from doing to the utmost by want of physical strength. After the birth of her little one she was naturally interested in all the problems of motherhood, and she reorganized, in the church, a "Mothers' Meeting," which had fallen into neglect.

In an informal way, the topics which are so interesting to mothers, were discussed. Many who had the privilege of attending those meetings, still recall Mrs. Thwing's helpful talks there, and the bright way in which she related some of her own experiences.

It was found that owing to home cares and outside engagements, the ladies of the parish could not sustain, with success, two distinct meetings. On this account the Mothers' Meeting was merged, after a while, in the Ladies' Prayer Meeting, which, of course, included others besides the mothers of the parish.

These meetings were fairly attended and were very interesting, especially those in which Mrs. Thwing took part. We were always sure to receive from her a clear interpretation of the passage of Scripture we were considering. Her mind seemed to grasp every phase of the subject, and her terse words often flashed a new light upon what had before seemed obscure. As one of her friends remarked, "a few words from her meant so much."

Her heart was with the Sewing Circle and she was present at the meetings whenever possible. She had to be excused from much active work there, as she was never physically strong, and the ladies were glad to have her reserve her strength for lines of work that were fully as helpful to the church.

The love and appreciation of the Sewing Circle was shown by the gift to Mrs. Thwing of a silk quilt, each lady furnishing the material and making a block for its completion. The time of presenting the gift was opportune, for it was given her when suffering from an attack of illness. She assured one of the ladies that it gave her no end of diversion to look it over, while convalescing, and to speculate upon whose hand made each particular block. Very soon after coming to the parish Mrs. Thwing took an active interest in the Sunday-school and became the teacher there of a class of young ladies. Mrs. Frank Foxcroft, who was principal of the Primary Department at the time, had long felt the need of an Intermediate Department. She thought that Primary scholars, graduated into that department, would receive instruction there which would better fit them for entering the main school.

Mrs. Thwing fully shared in this belief, and took such active measures that an Intermediate Department was successfully organized in the fall of the year 1884.

She at once assumed the duties of principal, and although it was an extra strain upon her limited strength, she loved the work more and more as the time passed.

Before going abroad with her husband, in 1885, she was careful to provide a substitute, so that the work of the department might be carried on in her absence. She remembered "the dear boys and girls," as she was wont to call them, by sending them messages, and sometimes a letter, to be read to them in the Sunday-school. This kind thought of them was keenly appreciated by her charge, and they gave her a royal welcome on her return. A special programme was prepared as a surprise, and Mrs. Thwing was deeply touched by these tokens of affection.

She again assumed her place in the school, but after serving them only one Sunday she was obliged, by ill health, again to place the work in the hands of her substitute. Before her entire recovery Mr. Thwing received and accepted a call to the Plymouth Church, Minneapolis, so that she never resumed the work. The Intermediate Department always retained a warm place in her heart, and it still exists a power for good in the North Avenue Church.

Conspicuous among the objects of Christian work which Mrs. Thwing was glad to aid, was the missionary cause, both Home and Foreign. In the first year of her connection with the church she became a member of the Auxiliary of the Woman's Board, formed by a union of the Shepherd and North Avenue Churches of Cambridge.

That she felt a growing interest in the work was shown by her increased subscriptions from year to year, and by consenting to serve as the First Directress of the

Auxiliary. The meetings were held, alternately, in each church, and it was Mrs. Thwing's duty to take charge of those held in her own church.

She made her little daughter, Mary, a member of the Auxiliary at the age of twenty months, and she became herself a Life Member of the Woman's Board. That the daughter might share equally with her mother in this honor, the Sunday-school made Mary also a Life Member. Her love for this cause never ceased, and one of her bequests was the sum of a thousand dollars to this Board.

While the Foreign work appealed thus largely to her sympathies, Mrs. Thwing was none the less interested in Home Missions. The Woman's Home Missionary Association, to which the Sewing Circle of the North Avenue Church became an Auxiliary, shared equally in her interest with that of the Woman's Board. She was glad to assist in its work, both by becoming one of its officers, and by the contribution of literary articles. One of these papers upon Missions in New Mexico was thought so opportune that it was printed as a tract by the Association and sent forth for wide circulation. She was Vice-President of the Association from 1882 to 1889, and the report for 1883 has this item :

"Mrs. Thwing, of Cambridge, made a special plea for an enlarged treasury, in view of the great demand for schools and missionaries among the ignorant of our land.''

At the Third Annual Meeting of the Woman's Home Missionary Association, in November, 1883, the ''Work at Home'' for that year gives the following extract from her public address :

''Mrs. Charles F. Thwing, of Cambridge, followed Miss Wakefield with what she said might be called an ungracious message, and yet she thought it ought not to be so called. The sacrifice which giving involves, is almost the only one now left to us as Christians, and we ought to hold on to that with tremendous energy. We must regard this money that we give, not as so many dollars and cents, but as the embodiment of so much moral power. It has mouths to speak, it has feet to run, it has hands to work; shall this be given to self or to Christ?

''The opportunities which are now open to us become responsibilities, and responsibilities which must be immediately assumed. What is done must be done quickly; a few years will decide whether our country shall be Christ's, or Anti-Christ's. This is a personal question, a question which every one of us must answer.''

This forceful appeal was listened to with great interest, and the ladies of her own church who were present, felt a pardonable pride in the able manner with which their pastor's wife handled her subject.

Without neglecting, as we have seen, any of these lines of Christian service, Mrs. Thwing proved herself a most diligent woman from the fact that she accomplished so much literary work. For this she was especially fitted by her natural tastes and by her college training.

She was the author of six articles which appeared in the Boston Journal upon the different texts or versions of Scripture from which scholars, at that time, were making their revision of the translation. These articles were complete and scholarly, showing careful study and deep research.

It was during her residence in Cambridge, that Mrs. Thwing assisted her father, Mr. Francis Gould Butler, in writing the history of Farmington, Maine. Its excellence as a local history is well known, and the help she thus gave her father was to her a labor of love.

She was ever interested in the literary subjects which occupied her husband. It was during his pastorate in Cambridge that they, together, prepared the volume entitled, "The Family—An Historical and Social Study." She also wrote editorials for the Golden Rule on many different subjects. That some of these were educational, goes without saying, for in educational matters she took a lively interest. In addition to her parish calls she often visited the public schools and sometimes gave talks to the children.

In whatever plans were made for the young people, she took a genuine interest, and those who were then boys and girls remember her with affection.

During the last part of Mrs. Thwing's stay in Cambridge a cooking school was established under the supervision of the Woman's Christian Temperance Union. She was greatly interested in this and entered into the work with zeal. The school was opened in that part of Cambridge known as "Dublin." Its aim was to teach the women of that locality how to prepare better food for their families. This work among such a rough people proved too exacting, and Mrs. Thwing was obliged, ere long, to give up her share of the labor into other hands.

Although she was not physically able to do all she wished, she was always ready with words of kindness and sympathy. In such interviews she had the courage of her convictions, and was always just in her decisions in regard to right and wrong. One of her most intimate friends writes: "She was so true to herself that even in her love and sympathy for her best friends she would not sacrifice one whit of the truth." Her personality was very strong and it was her great charm, but back of all this was a character so well balanced, a brain so active, and a heart so true, that nothing could unhinge her.

To this friend Mrs. Thwing was especially helpful, and she testified that ever since their association in Cambridge she has always written to her "for help over the hard places."

When his people heard of Mr. Thwing's decision to accept his call to Plymouth Church, Minneapolis, there was universal sorrow among them. It was hard to lose one whose ministry had been so acceptable, and so fruitful of good results. It was also hard to give up to another parish, one who had so endeared herself as the pastor's co-worker.

Previous to entering their new field of work, Mr. and Mrs. Thwing spent a few weeks at her father's home in Farmington, Maine. While there the house was destroyed by a fire which swept away a large part of the village. Through this trying time Mrs. Thwing was calm and self-reliant, and when it was known that the house must burn, she worked to the last moment in helping to save their valuables.

When the time came for Mr. and Mrs. Thwing's departure to Minneapolis, a goodly number of their Cambridge friends went to the station in Boston to see them off on the outgoing train. Without any of them knowing of the other's intention, each of these friends brought something in the way of refreshment for the travelers. The seats about them were piled high with good things, and they were deeply touched at this expression of love from so many of the dear people whom they were leaving. Mrs. Thwing seemed to take away with her nothing but pleasant memories of Cambridge.

In letters to her friends there were frequent expressions of her great love for the old home. "We were so happy," she writes, "those seven years, and we are so happy now, in all the friendships there formed."

Another time she writes, "I wonder if you have any idea how proud I am of the continued love and remembrances of my Cambridge friends."

"The dear church is never forgotten, God bless it, and all that love and labor for it."

It was gratifying to her Cambridge friends to hear how she still loved them, and to know that although, afterward, she formed the most pleasant associations, and met with the kindest of friends, she always retained a peculiar fondness for the city and church to which she came as a bride.

SARAH E. DAWES.

The Years in Minneapolis.

IN the fall of 1886 Mrs. Thwing came to Minneapolis with her husband as he entered upon his duties as pastor of Plymouth Church. She took up her share of the work with enthusiasm, aiding in all ways that she could.

Her keen, bright, cultivated and consecrated intellect, good judgment, and pleasant ways of meeting people fitted her to be a leader of rare power. Plymouth Church has had, in all its history, but slight experience of the blessing of a pastor's wife. We were very happy in the thought of having such an one come among us, who could help to fill out her husband's work in so many ways, touching, as she could, lines of activity for which he could find neither time nor opportunity, and making friends with a large circle.

One of the crying needs of the church at that stage of its history, was some power that should draw its members together in living fellowship. This work, the new pastor and his wife set themselves earnestly to do. In all social gatherings she was a power, winning all by her brightness and cordiality. She received many calls during that first winter, and made many, and somehow got a hold on people who had been slipping out of the fold. It was wonderful how she and her husband managed to remember the names and faces of so many people, and there is nothing more winning to the ordinary mortal than the compliment of being remembered from a mere introduction. She has explained that this seeming triumph of genius was really the genius of taking pains, and how they used to recall to each other, after a social gathering, names, and faces, and dress, and try to fix some peg to hang a memory to.

She was a great help in the Women's Meetings of the church, attending when she could, and speaking most effectively upon occasion. An address of hers at a Union Missionary gathering is still recalled, when she spoke with great power on the consecration of wealth to the Lord.

She aimed to keep in touch with all the work of the church, rather than to give herself to any one branch, thinking she could thus best aid her husband. Her voice was often heard in the church prayer-meeting, and always with acceptance. Such gifts of mind and heart fitted her to be a leader in the church and community. Could she have done nothing more, it was much to have such a woman stand at her husband's side in full and beautiful accord with him and his work, and a constant strength and inspiration to him.

Would that health might have been hers, also. That, coming a stranger to the place, she could have made a deep impression in the brief months that it was given to her to work, proves her power.   For, as so many times before in her life, ill health blighted her hopes and ambitions. Even what she was able to do, was done in weariness and painfulness.   After a few months her health broke down completely, and during almost the remainder of her husband's residence in Minneapolis, she was either a shut-in invalid at home, or away seeking health.

To a comparatively few was it given to know her large gifts and loving heart.   Such a life carries with it a special plea for immortality.   It was planned on too large a scale to come to its best amid the limitations of this life.   The fine intellect that was always cramped and hindered by a weak and suffering body, must somewhere be able to work out its thoughts freely and fully.   For her, we think of death as but a portal into larger life. There, all beautiful promise of mind and soul shall have its fruition, and we doubt not that in the "many mansions" she finds opportunity to use all gifts and graces of mind and character among those who "serve Him."

MARY T. HALE.

The Years in Cleveland.

WHEN, in 1890, the Western Reserve University welcomed a new President, Cleveland Vassar Alumnae were glad to find in the wife of President Thwing a former college acquaintance and friend. Having been introduced in the winter of 1877, in Boston, to Carrie Butler, I was glad to find, in 1890, that the person whom I had always remembered for her bright and cordial manners, was Mrs. Thwing, and that she was now one of our Cleveland college women. In the fourteen years that had elapsed since her college days, she had lost none of her college enthusiasm or ideals, and brought to her Cleveland life singularly strong college spirit and interest. She entered heart and soul into her husband's work as the President of a large and growing university. She had a rare appreciation of all the elements that tend to strengthen the foundation and growth of the different departments of a university. Where some women are narrow and contracted in their views and, therefore, in the advice they give, she was always broad, with a very just estimate of relative values.

A university founded in a city needs to be popular with the home institutions, if it is to have as large a field for usefulness as is possible. Mrs. Thwing joined with her husband in appreciating all the elements of strength in a city like Cleveland, and always delighted to honor and commend every influence that tended toward helping and supporting the university. She had rare judgment, rare common sense, rare business sagacity, rare and sterling integrity. From the first all persons were her friends, because she had the power of keeping friends. In true friendship one never measures what is given and taken, and delights only in giving. When one who knew Mrs. Thwing well thinks of her, one must always accord to her the highest honor in friendship, that of having been a true friend.

In her relations to the students of the university, she at once took an active part. With her husband, she met the students at various receptions and banquets and was always a bright and ready hostess. She took particular interest in each and every student, gathering and keeping in her mind various incidents of college history peculiar to each. When a student had graduated and gone, if the name was mentioned by professor or instructor, there would come a ready response with some kindly anecdote, showing the clear and definite impression that each one had left with her. Most of us realize, I think, that such memory and interest come only from rare, unselfish appreciation and a personal sense of responsibility.

One never approached Mrs. Thwing with the case of an individual student who needed help, in money or other ways, without being sure of a ready and responsive listener and a willing helper. The rare opportunities for helping which appeal to the President's family in university matters, were never lightly regarded by Mrs. Thwing or considered as tiresome and uninteresting. She realized fully that each individual case was as important to the person concerned as if there were not hundreds of just such cases, and always gave untiring interest, sympathy and help. Universities are often spoken of as corporations, as something devoid of a soul. That was not Mrs. Thwing's conception of a university, and as far as possible she gave to all that came within her reach the touch of life that institutions as well as individuals need.

Mrs. Thwing met the women of her own College, Vassar, soon after coming to the city, when, at her request, a reception was given for them at the College for Women. All were delighted with her cordial and hearty interest in all college questions. She was, a little later, a guest at a Vassar dinner at the Hollenden, and I remember hearing her say as we left the hotel, "Are not college reunions delightful?"

Although doing so much, in time, money and thought, for her husband's university, she never forgot her allegiance to the numerous activities in which Vassar women manifest their loyalty. She was a member of the Vassar Students' Aid Society and was especially interested in the completion of the Maria Mitchell Endowment Fund. She never ceased to value the sound training given to Vassar women in the early days of that college under President Raymond, and to hope for all college women equally strong training. By her influence in Western Reserve University she did much to make possible for women the highest and best culture.

I am glad to remember Mrs. Thwing as a Vassar woman, and to think that a mind peculiarly fair and just in its estimates, had its college training under Vassar's roof.

Two children were born to Mrs. Thwing in Cleveland—one a son, Francis Butler Thwing, born in February, 1891, the other a daughter, Apphia, born in August, 1892. If one thought he had sounded the depths of her nature in considering and discussing with her educational interests, he had only to talk with her concerning children and home life to see the height and breadth and depth of her heart and mind. Here again, in spite of a nature naturally impulsive and exceedingly easily moved, she was sound and true in her estimates, broad in her views, tender and loyal in her considerations of children's interests and rights. She was eminently philosophical and reasonable, and considerate of every phase of child study. She was, with her husband, one of the founders of the Froebel School in Cleveland, a school which brings as fine teaching, proportionately, into the kindergarten and primary, as one usually finds in the highest departments of universities.

Her ready answer, when asked to join the Daughters of the American Revolution, because it gave such an interest in one's ancestors, was, "But I am much more interested in my descendants than in my ancestors."

I happened to discuss corporal punishment with her one day. She did not believe in it even for small children, but did believe in reasoning, as with older persons, and that children were as capable of being reasoned with as their elders. This she always did, and in her children's minds must remain a distinct image of one who never coerced, who encouraged and waited for the fulfillment of her expectations in their conduct.

All the interests of her children, whether play or work, were her own interests. When her daughter Mary, now a Sophomore in college, entered the Central High School in this city, her mother went with her and spent the entire morning in seeing her registered and

noting classifications, grades and systems with as much
interest as if personally connected with the institution.
Such intelligent appreciation and sympathy in educational
work is a very pleasant sight in this century of hurry,
bustle and carelessness about personal obligations. I
mention this one incident because it was so characteristic
of Mrs. Thwing's appreciation of her children's life.

A group of six or seven ladies in Cleveland formed,
four years ago, a Mothers' Club. Mrs. Thwing took a
great interest in their meetings and talks and contributed,
I am told, most valuable suggestions and experiences.
The members of this club were most sincerely attached
to one another. Their common interest in children
and child questions and problems drew them close
together.

Although Mrs. Thwing's residence in Cleveland
covered the short period of eight years, she had made her
influence felt in many more directions than those simply
of her home, church and university circles.

When any question of public interest arose in the
city, it always found a sympathetic and respectful sup-
porter in Mrs. Thwing. She had a true New England
conception of the close relation which all civic interests
should hold to the various households and individuals of
the city. When the law was passed in Columbus giving
women in Ohio the privilege of voting on all matters per-

taining to schools, the women of Cleveland gave a banquet in honor of the senators and legislators from Cleveland who had supported the law. Among the most prominent speakers of Cleveland, Mrs. Thwing responded to a toast and won hosts of friends by her clear and eloquent account of the workings of such a system in Boston, and the statement of her belief in the value of the expressed intelligence of women in school matters. Any one who saw her as she spoke that night will always remember the dignity and power with which she stated her thoughts, and the charm of her manner in speaking.

In church affiliations, she was a member and interested worker in the Euclid Avenue Congregational Church. She was always ready to help any poor and struggling church, and having been asked to give money to aid in starting a new Congregational church, before promising her offering, drove to the locality, examined the need in that community of another church, and then gave willingly the sum desired. This was a fair example of a characteristic trait. She was generous, but always where she thought her generosity would not be wasted.

She had a happy way of greeting members that assemble at receptions given by the university. Singularly quick in repartee, there was always a ready answer for each new comer in the long line of guests. Few women have the power to interest themselves in so many; few women, who have the power, have the inclination to exert it. For interest, genuine kindly interest in others' occupations and welfare requires true unselfishness on the part of the one manifesting it.

Sincerity and unselfishness were prominent traits in Mrs. Thwing's character. She looked for the best in each; she had the magnetic power which brings the best in each to the surface. Possessed of a great sense of humor, she always saw the weakness of human nature, but with no unpleasant feeling. She was good company in a rare sense, because she loved humanity in itself. She manifested in herself the best elements of New England ancestry and training, united with the kindness and tolerance that broaden any nature.

She had fine discrimination in literature, and this was always apparent in her conversation.

Her home shows the nature of the one who planned and furnished it. In it are reflected her brightness and taste. She shaped her life on high and lofty ideals, her thoughts were noble, her actions sincere and honorable. Such a life, whether short or long in years, is long in the beneficent influence which it leaves in family, university, church and community.

Emma M. Perkins.

Journal of a Tour in Europe.

1885.

EDINBURGH, 26 July, 1885.

Events have been so crowded and impressions so many and so strange that it is difficult to recall events or analyze impressions. The voyage, begun at 9:30, July 11, and finished at about the same hour July 21, was monotonous, and yet in many ways it was all we could have asked. It did not add to our list of friends, hardly to that of acquaintances, unless I except a very remarkable man, ———— by name, plumber by trade, trigomist by profession. He has had three excellent wives whom he tires not of extolling, and they together with his feats in plumbing formed the staple relaxation of the voyage. He is a type of a self-made man, egotistic, aggressive, self-poised, yet whole hearted and generous. He might have sat for Howells' Silas Lapham, except that a religious faith has refined certain coarse features of the successful Colonel.

Liverpool we found smoky and dirty, a true commercial city which was more honored by our immediate departure than it could have been by our staying. We fled to Chester. And what shall I say of Chester? What shall I not say of Chester? Of her delightful Queen Hotel, where we ate our strawberries and cream by an open door leading out into a charming old-fashioned garden with marigolds and primroses; what of her quaint shops and streets, her queer houses, her ancient walls, her grand cathedral? Our first view was obtained by a ride perched on top of a tram car. This procedure did not bring us into close association with the nobility and gentry but accomplished our purpose of getting an idea of the town. We left the car at the river and wandered about the castle by the Dee, then up into the town and through the curious rows to the Cathedral. Grand, grand old church, a fitting temple for God and for man's worship. The service was read in the Lady Chapel at half-past five and we stayed and bowed with the worshipers assembled. The dreary sing-song monotone of the reader and the responses chanted by the choir turned into mechanism the wonderful, almost inspired, words of the service. The singing of the general confession seemed almost blasphemous. But in the vaulted arches themselves seemed to be worship without words. It is wonderful to me how men of that rude age could so make stone praise God. Infinity and aspiration! No one can enter and not feel them.

We went home. It seemed a little primitive to take a candle; to find no spring bed. But we were in a condition to declare that gas and spring beds were vulgar modern innovations. I am not sure but that gas would have seemed an anachronism after such an afternoon.

An early rise, an early breakfast and a comfortable cab, and half-past eight found us bowling away towards Hawarden Castle, the home of Mr. Gladstone, six or eight miles away in Flintshire, Wales. We found the same beautiful, level, cultivated country through which the cars brought us to Chester. Everywhere the eye is charmed by the evident thrift, the substantial character of every man-made object, be it causeway or church, and by the taste and beauty with which everything is planned and decorated. The miles of hawthorn hedge, interwoven with ivy, roses and honeysuckle growing wild, were a charm to one to whom all these are exotics. The Hawarden estate embraces a territory ten miles by eight. We rode a mile perhaps after passing the gate before reaching the house. Its grounds seemed to be in a state of nature and could hardly have yielded much revenue. The mansion, solid, substantial, like everything else, was yet fine. In the old Castle, however, we found our richest treat. All of Scott's novels came trooping before my mind as we explored moat and drawbridge, keep and battlement and dungeon. It is only a ruin, but singularly picturesque, clothed with the all-covering ivy. Our conductor was a Welshman ardently attached to the family. With pride he showed us an enormous oak, not less than three and one-half feet in diameter at the butt, which was felled by the united force of the male Gladstones: "Master Gladstone, Master William Henry, Master Henry Neville, Master Stephen E. and Master somebody else." "Master Gladstone," he said, "has given up the estate to Master William Henry, who is his heir, and best of all Master William Henry has an heir born last week." The old man's joy illustrated the strength of English family pride. Pointing to the windows of Gladstone's library the guide said: "ten thousand volumes, sir, and master of every one of them." He was very loquacious as he dilated on the past and present glories of the place, although we understood his rapid delivery with difficulty. Indeed, the first days we were in England we doubted whether we understood the English language at all. We are now conceited enough to believe that it is we who speak English with purity. In the first place the names of many common objects are different. Mews for stables, tariff for rate, passage for ticket, guard for conductor, luggage van for baggage car, underdone for rare,—and many more. We also notice that each class of persons seems to have a different accent. The cabmen speak differently from waiters, the waiters from shop-keepers, the shop-keepers from railroad men, and so on with this remarkable distinction, the higher up the social scale we go the more they *talk like Americans.* The cabman we had at Glasgow we simply gave up trying to understand.

The Scotch, of course, have quite another dialect. The driver who took us through the Lake District complimented me by saying that I spoke very good English, better than any American he had ever seen, and he should have thought me to be an English lady!

Getting back to Chester at about quarter-past eleven, we were driven at once to the Cathedral where we had tickets to an oratorio. It happened to be the triennial festival, and a choir of three hundred voices with a picked orchestra performed Gounod's Redemption. We enjoyed it intensely, although the vast spaces of the Cathedral doubtless aided more the sentimental than the artistic performance. The oratorio loses, in comparison with Handel's Messiah, in the substitution of weak paraphrases for the grand words of holy writ. The recitative also grew monotonous. As I look back upon it, I find it is the orchestral rather than the vocal parts which linger in my memory, while with the Messiah the reverse is the case. But it was a great privilege. We took lunch in the interval of the oratorio, and it was half-past three when we left the Cathedral for a walk round the walls and a visit to the water tower. It was said that the Bishop of Chester (Dr. Stubbs) does not approve these concerts in the Cathedral and departs to the remotest corner of his diocese at the time they are given. Dean Howson, however, was present.

To go back to the water tower. The inevitable three-pence opened for us a museum which contained a strange jumble of alligators' skins and elephant's teeth with some objects of real interest. In the dungeon of this tower the Earl of Derby's daughters, hostages for Charles I, were confined. Looking down on the yard below the tower were the remains of a Roman temple, of which the pillars had been dug up in the town and brought here and erected in what is believed to be their original positions. The Phoenix tower, between the Cathedral and the water tower, bears this inscription:

"King Charles I. stood on this tower and saw his
army defeated at Rowlin Moor, Sept. 24, 1645."

Walking round the walls we soon came to the river Dee at the point spanned by the Grosvenor bridge, one long, magnificent arch, the finest in England. Here a tram car was taken and brought us to the Queen's just in time to get our train for Windermere. This ride through Cheshire, Lancashire and Westmoreland was a constant charm. The country seemed like one vast park. The miles of haw-thorn hedge intergrown with wild roses, poppies, honey-suckle and daisies, as well as the neat stone houses and barns covered with ivy and roses, were a delight to the eye. We saw only peace and prosperity.

The little we have traveled on English railroads leads to the conclusion that they are not so well conducted as our own. The people do not seem to understand how to get a train off, and in three out of five of the trips we have taken the trains have been late. From Chester they were late in starting. We find second class carriages very good. The first class are not fine. They are up-holstered in broadcloth, while second class have terry or something of that kind. None of the carriages are too neat and none approach the comfort of our common car, much less that of the Pullman. The system of carriages has some advantages over cars, particularly when you have a compartment alone or with an agreeable com-panion. It gives one a helpless feeling, however, to be locked in, and on the whole I prefer the American system, especially were I traveling alone should I desire it.

A *bus* ride from Windermere brought us to Bowness, a mile and a half away, and the Old England opened its charmingly hospitable doors. This is a true English inn, plain and neat, yet thoroughly homelike and com-fortable. Its grounds slope to Lake Windermere, and there one finds numerous pleasure boats for rowing.

We were now in the Lake District, with beauties of art and nature around us, with associations of poetry and romance thronging upon us,—and one day for all. I think we made a wise choice. In the morning we went into the little village church. Like all village churches that we have passed, it is a low-bowed massive structure with

square tower. One really fine window from Furness
Abbey adorns it. It is very plain to see what a powerful
influence the church wields in these communities. The
church is the central object in every town. It is always
ancient, venerable and venerated. Some way England
strikes us as a more Christian country than America.
Certainly it bears the marks of a more Christian country.
We have not failed to find a Bible in every room we have
occupied. In several places Scripture texts have adorned
the walls. Tracts and sometimes scrolls are in the railroad stations. But, most of all, the church seems to be
the pivotal point around which the lives of these towns
move. Notices of all kinds are posted in the vestibules.
I noticed in a wee church at Wythburn a notice for a
meeting for licensing the sale of beer, wine, etc. The
question has occurred to me are there not many disad-
vantages connected with the severance of church and
state? The perpetuation of the church and of church
ordinances with us depends upon the liberality of the few.
We can't build or support cathedrals or parish schools.

A ride on the steamer from Bowness brought us to
Ambleside where we bargained with an intelligent young
fellow to drive us to Keswick and the Falls of Lodore.
The region through which we passed was very pretty.
While the lakes are smaller and the mountains lower
than at home, we were obliged to confess that the effect

was charming and beyond our anticipation. The mountains are thrown together in reckless confusion, seemingly piled and jumbled without design. On our way to Keswick we rode under the "dark brow of the mighty Helvellyn." Scott's words seem to fit the gloomy towering mountain as no others could. We skirted the little lakes of Grasmere, Rydal, and Thirby and struck the beautiful Derwentwater just before we reached Keswick. The whole ride bristled with interesting memories or associations. In the little churchyard at Ambleside lay the mortal of Harriet Martineau and of Dr. Arnold, while just beyond were the Knoll and Fox How, the houses made immortal as their residences. Rydal Mount, the home of Wordsworth, a substantial stone house with well kept grounds, lay just beyond. In the churchyard of the little village at Grasmere we found the grave of Wordsworth, marked by a plain slate slab bearing the words,

WILLIAM WORDSWORTH,
1850.

Within the church a marble tablet to the memory of the great poet is placed, simple and elegant. It is this:

"A true philosopher and poet, who, by the special gift and calling of Almighty God, whether he discoursed of man or nature, failed not to lift up the heart to holy things; tired not of maintaining the cause of the poor and simple, and so in perilous times was raised up to be a chief minister, not only of noblest poesy, but of high and sacred truth."

Upon a stone marking the grave of one of his little children were these lines:

"Six months to six years added he remained
Upon this sinful earth by sin unstained.
O blessed Lord, whose mercy thus removed
A child, whom every eye that looked on loved,
Support us, teach us calmly to resign,
What we possessed and now is wholly thine."

At Wythburn we took a little lunch in an English bar room, and, while the horse was resting, went into a tiny church, said to be one of the smallest in the kingdom. Like all churches it was venerable and solid, though of the plainest possible description. To the readers of Wordsworth it is known as the "Wee, modest house of prayer."

A little thing interested me very much as showing the regard of even the common people of England for historical associations. The driver pointed out a considerable heap of stones which he said was believed to mark the grave of one of the Cumberland Kings before the consolidation of the counties. The pile of stones had lain there for centuries, and yet miles of stone wall had been built about it without one of these tributes to the memory of that ancient monarch being disturbed.

Lodore we reached by driving through Keswick round the other side of Derwentwater, by a romantic road underneath wild overhanging crags. Low water robbed the falls of its grandeur, but it was still beautiful, flowing down its hundred feet of rock-worn path. It must justify in its full glory every one of Southey's adjectives.

A plain, rather too plain, house awaited us, and after tea we sallied out to find Southey's home and grave. We plainly see that we are in a northern latitude by the long twilight. We can read in the house at nine o'clock. The Crosthwaite Parish church in the outskirts of the town was the first object of our pilgrimage. This venerable church belonged to a very early date, although its two sides show marked differences in architecture and probably belong to different periods. Within its walls lies a marble effigy of the poet, while a plain sarcophagus marks his grave in the churchyard. Returning we sat upon a seat in the stone wall and watched the sun set behind the "westermost Wythop." Climbing a slight eminence on our left brought us to Greta Hall where Southey had his home and where Coleridge was his guest for several years. A young ladies' boarding school now occupies its spacious halls.

A quarter to eight on Friday found us on our way northward. At Carlisle we took two hours for the Cathedral. In one of the aisles repose the remains of my old friend Paley, and over his grave I stood thinking what if I were to strike my foot against a watch. Some friends to do him honor (?) in 1876, removed the pulpit in which he used to preach and substituted a carved marble pulpit. In the north transept is a large stained glass window inserted to the memory of the five children of Archbishop Tait, who died in the adjoining Abbey while he was Dean of Carlisle. At Carlisle is a window just put in by officers, singularly beautiful, representing Joshua, Gideon and Maccabaeus, the warrior Israelites. The east window, put in in the 14th century is said to be one of the finest windows in the kingdom, but we found ourselves unable to appreciate it. It is immense in size and mixed and minute in design.

Glasgow, like Liverpool, bears the marks of a commercial city, smoky and dirty. We were most unfortunate in our selection of a hotel, and we left early the morning after our arrival rather cross. But we paid our respects to the truly grand old Cathedral which stands in a perfect state, and is wonderfully embellished by its exquisite windows. Each cathedral boasts some preeminence. Glasgow claims the most perfect crypt in existence. And wonderful indeed are the underground churches, perfect in their architecture, pure Gothic and decorated with exquisite windows. A window representing our Saviour gave to me the most perfect idea of how he might have looked, of any picture I have ever seen. It was the work of the Munich Art School. It was in these crypts where Sir Walter Scott places the meeting between Rob Roy and Frank Osbaldistone. The metropolis with its commanding statue of Knox lay back of the Cathedral, the old Barony church close by its side.

Friday, July 24, we spent in the Scottish lakes, our course being Glasgow to Balloch by rail passing Dumbarton; Balloch to Inversnaid by steamer on Loch Lomond, Inversnaid to Sconachlacher by coach, five miles, lunch there and then steamer on Loch Katrine to the Trossachs, through the Trossachs and by coach to Callendar, Callendar by rail to Edinburgh. The day was warm and the jaunt too long. On boat and coach I was made miserable by smoke. The tobacco of Scotland is the vilest I ever smelled, and pipes are the rule. I was in torture from the Trossachs to Callendar while five out of eleven passengers puffed clouds of vilest smoke into face, eyes and nostrils. The smoking habit seems to divest a man of all regard for the rights and feelings of others.

On the whole Scotland has hardly charmed us as much as England. The country is rougher and less cultivated. The scenery in the Scottish lakes disappointed us and we felt quite willing to place Rangeley beside it. Yet it must be admitted Loch Lomond is beautiful. Its surface was not glaring as was that of Windermere the day we crossed it. That peculiar glassiness I never remember to have seen before.

Our first view of Edinburgh completely charmed us, and the charm was never broken during the few days of our stay. I have serious doubts whether the pleasant days at Edinburgh will be duplicated during our trip. We took rooms at the Cockburn House close to the station, and in walking to them the picturesque features of the old city burst upon us at once. At our right were the beautiful Princess gardens stretching down the ravine dividing the old city from the new until they meet the remarkable massive Greek stone buildings occupied by the Antiquarian Museum and the National Portrait Gallery. In front of us was piled up the old city, house upon house, tier upon tier, up the side of what must have been a precipice. First impressions are strong, still I can conceive of no circumstances in which Edinburgh would not have appealed to us as singularly attractive. Upon Sunday I was prepared to rest, and damp and misty weather setting in, there was little to tempt me out. In the morning, however, we worshiped at St. Andrews Free Church. I say worshiped, but there was very little element of worship in the bare service. No organ, no fine hymns, but only a miserable transcription of the psalms beside which Dr. Watts is as Homer. Everything about the place was as bare and stiff as the service. The seats were high, straight-backed boxes with fast-closed doors. The sermon was by Principal Rainy, the chief antagonist of Robertson Smith. It was delivered without notes and was a clear and forcible exposition of the truths taught in the parable of the sower.

We walked up to St. Giles Cathedral, where John Knox held forth in the stormy days of Scotland's history, if indeed Scotland can be said to have any days that were not stormy. Like all cathedrals it has been the work of different ages, the oldest parts dating back to the year of 1120. Its history is closely interwoven with that of the country. It was partially burned during the wars with England. In it are buried Murray and Montrose. Here on the 23d July, 1637, the Dean (James Hanna) read the English service book, the first and last time it was ever read in St. Giles. The Dean received a stool at his head and was glad to retire. This lack of knowledge of the Scottish people on the part of Charles I., who sought to change the religion of a country by a proclamation, illustrates the character of the man and of those methods which cost him his life. In this church also James VI. bade his people good-bye upon his departure to assume the crown of England. There is something very beautiful to me in the way the life of these people is written in these churches.

The Parliament House which stands by the side of St. Giles brought us into close touch with the history of the country. Some indifferent portraits of distinguished citizens were its chief interest. In the square separating the two buildings, formerly the churchyard, lies the remains of the man who swayed the history of Scotland in its crucial year. "I. K., 1572," is the only inscription. I can not love him, stern, unloving man that he was, but the times needed him and the results of his work have been for the welfare of his land and the honor of his Lord.

The old Tolbooth prison, made famous by Scott, stood close to the Cathedral. It is gone now, but a heart laid in the brick pavement marks its site as the Heart of Mid-Lothian. Walking down High street we passed the Canongate Tolbooth, where Montrose was imprisoned. Crossing the bridge we took a car at the Postoffice, made a circuit of the town, and got home in time for dinner. Our ardor not in the least quenched, we sallied out after dinner and walked down to the Grassmarket, the scene of the Porteus riot. The place looked innocent enough, yet it required but little imagiination to bring back the scenes of that night. We found ourselves near the castle, and a long climb up a dirty close brought us to the summit of the hill it crowns. We got a little idea of how the poor people live by our walk through the close. Poverty here, as everywhere, is dirty and degrading. Yet in Edinburgh it seems to have some picturesque features. It is interesting to see the women and children come out of these closes into the main streets, as bees out of a hive, and sun themselves in the light of happier lives. The women, bareheaded, have their knitting in their hands and stand and talk together. The children, barefooted as well as bareheaded, play about. The streets in Edinburgh seem always full. The old fish-wives were quite a feature in their short skirts and with their masculine manners.

Tuesday morning we visited the Albert Memorial Statue which we found rather disappointing; but the National Picture Gallery well repaid a visit. It was very full in its productions of Scotch artists, Sir David Wilkie, Andrew Geddes and James Drummond. The scenes from Scotch history: Porteus Mob, Montrose, Mary Stuart's Abdication, etc., were strikingly executed. Several Van Dykes were well worth seeing.

At eleven o'clock we made a trip to Rosslyn Chapel and Castle, returning for dinner. This exquisite Chapel proved most interesting from an architectural point of view. Built in the fifteenth century, it presents an admirable example of the decorated Gothic. The carving is delicate and exhibits every variety possible of design. Each capital is different from every other. The Castle, a mere ruin, though picturesque, gave us some insight into the method of living in the feudal times. Two men ridiculously drunk were about the Castle. We have seen already more drunken men than I see in a year at home. Everybody seems to drink.

The evening we fulfilled a cherished plan of climbing Arthur's Seat and viewing Edinburgh by moonlight. The days are so very long here that we did not start until after half-past eight. The ride took us by Holyrood and round the Salisbury Craig. A wonderful Craig this which sits as a crown upon the brow of the hill. We wound round the hill watching the rising moon and the flicker of the gas lights as they appeared in the houses of the city. We passed St. Leonard's and Jennie Dean's cottage, saw Craig Millar in the distance and the house where Prince Charles slept the night before Prestonpans. The ascent to Arthur's Seat after leaving the carriage proved too much and we were obliged to content ourselves with a view from a less lofty height. Beautiful indeed was the city lying beneath us, with the fine old Castle in the centre, the delicate spire of the Scott monument rising to its height, the lights glowing and sparkling from window and from street.

Wednesday morning we visited Holyrood. To this I had looked forward with the greatest interest. The palace is rather imposing from without but most bare and cheerless within. Finished in the plainest style, it bears no vestige of magnificence or royalty. Its rooms, all suggestive of sorrow, treachery and crime, are not pleasant. It has seemed easier in Scotland than anywhere else to forgive Mary Stuart her crimes, and to execrate her enemies and the times in which she lived. The chapel, a mere ruin, sown with the dust of many Scottish kings, had some architectural interest.

I must speak of a curious incident which the guide at Edinburgh Castle told us as he showed us the room where James VI. was born. He says, in 1818, when the authorities were repairing the walls of that room, a coffin was found in which were the remains of an infant wrapped in royal robes. The coffin plate bore the initial "I." Query: Who was the child?

The Abbey Hotel at Melrose received us, and our room looked directly upon a wall of the old ruin. A ride of five miles brought us to the Tweed, which crossing, we came to Dryburgh Abbey, a somber, desolate spot. Here Sir Walter Scott has found a resting place among the ashes of his ancestors. The birds have built their nests above him and keep loving watch over his tomb. The Monastery here was the best preserved we have seen and gave us a good idea of the life of mingled jollity and asceticism.

Melrose by moonlight! It was a little disappointing. The moon was slow in rising and at eleven was not far above the horizon. It was a weird and melancholy sight to see those massive piles of stone standing alone and speaking so eloquently of the times that are no more. The old cathedrals are to me very inspiring. I love to think of the long centuries in which the light of Christian truth which they have held aloft has never been extinguished. But the ruins of a cathedral are unutterable melancholy.

An early start in the morning gave us a visit to Abbotsford and brought us back to Melrose for the eleven o'clock train to Durham. Some of the curiosities at Abbotsford interested us greatly. Such was the crucifix held in the hand of Mary, Queen of Scots, before her execution. The ride to Durham was uninteresting and attended with some changes and delays. We arrived a little after four and walked directly to the Cathedral. It is beautifully situated on the bank of the river Wear, along whose bank, as seems common in England, runs a path. It was a steep climb which brought us to the Cathedral just as the afternoon service was over. This venerable church dates back to the latter part of the 11th century and retains much of the Norman work. In it repose the remains of St. Cuthbert at whose shrine the very stone was worn by the knees of worshiping pilgrims. The venerable Bede lies in the chapel at the rear of the church.

We reached Peterborough in the middle of the afternoon and took a *bus* to the Angel where we ordered dinner, and proceeded to the Cathedral. Our visit here was in some respects the most interesting of all those paid to the churches. The building was in process of repair. There were therefore few visitors and we had the verger to ourselves. The architecture of this Cathedral is particularly grand, of the late Norman style. The apse is very fine, while the vaulting of the Lady Chapel is exquisite. Here is the tomb of Catharine of Aragon, unmarked, and here also was buried Mary, Queen of Scots, until her removal to Westminster.

It was bed time when we reached Ely and the Lamb gave us a comfortable home for the night. The restorations of the Cathedral here are very complete. The stone is clean and pure and in its exhibitions of different styles of architecture this church is prominent. Its octagon lantern with its rich decorations is grand. Its two Chapels, Bishop Alcock's and Bishop West's, are excellent specimens of decorated and perpendicular architecture, both very rich.

Our first sight of London was at about two o'clock, Saturday, August 2nd. We rode from the Liverpool street station to Bloomsbury square, and thence to Camden for our trunk. Our room in Southampton street, which we had engaged in advance, we found three flights up and

very poor. It made us a little homesick, but the middle of
the next week we are to have two good rooms on the first
floor.   Breakfast and tea we take in our room and dinner
at a nice restaurant near by.   We have not been
over well pleased with English meals, particularly breakfast, at which it seems to be the custom to serve only
bread (cold) with chops or steak.   No potato, no breakfast cake, no porridge, no fruit. Butter is universally poor.
We have seen some good, and think ourselves fortunate
if it is not absolutely rank.   It does not seem to be the
fashion to give napkins except at dinner.   This was so in
Edinburgh.   Everything is eaten on one plate.   Roast
beef is almost invariably delicious. Steak is no better than
ours.   Prices we have found dear.   Breakfasts at hotels
have ranged from 2s.6d. to 3s.6d. and literally nothing
to eat but meat and cold bread.

We took a little walk on High Holborn and went
into some book shops, etc.   Everything seems intolerably
dirty.   The burning of soft coal gives everything a
grimy look and makes the air foul.   It seems impossible
to fill the lungs with pure air.   Sunday morning we
walked down to St. Margaret's church, near Westminster,
to hear Canon Farrar preach.   It was a very unpleasant
walk, through poverty, wretchedness and filth, foul
sights and foul smells.   The old church in which are
interred Sir Walter Raleigh and William Caxton presents

no remarkable features. A large, crowded house listened to the sermon which was on the things which cannot be shaken (Heb. xii: 27). He is a vigorous, energetic speaker, reminding one of Phillips Brooks, and showing himself to be the same master of phrases as a speaker, that we have found him to be as a writer. The service freed from the Cathedral mummeries was quite endurable. We took lunch at the Westminster Palace Hotel, and waited there until three o'clock when the service in the Abbey began. Canon Westcott spoke from the same text from which Farrar preached in the morning. He was very direct and vigorous. The testimony which he bore to the value of the Bible was striking, coming from so eminent a Biblical scholar. "The more I study the Bible, the more I find it the Word of God."

In the evening we heard Stopford A. Brooke, whose Bedford Chapel is near by. He had few hearers. Some way Unitarian Christianity does not attract the people. The service was similar to that of the Church of England with Christ left out of it. His subject was a very similar one to those of the morning. The sermon was strong, and yet weak, where Unitarianism is and must always be weak. It gave one nothing to rest on, but turned man back upon himself. The infallibility of the church is gone, the infallibility of the Bible is gone, man has no other rule than himself. Mr. Brooke has a peculiar manner, strong and forcible, yet with a little snarl in his voice.

Monday I found myself a good deal fagged and was quite willing Charles should go out alone to find the American minister and to do other necessary business. After dinner, however, I felt equal to some exertion and we visited the British Museum, which is close by.

The weather we are finding cold and stone buildings rather uncomfortable. Every morning is damp and cloudy with signs of rain, but before noon it clears away and is moderately pleasant. We took a hansom Tuesday and rode for an hour about the West End viewing the fine residences and the parks. Buckingham Palace did not look very attractive. In fact all the buildings are so smoked and grimed that none of them can be said to be really attractive. Hyde Park looked dreary. I expected flowers in it. Indeed in seeing everything there is a sense of disappointment which is hard to define. I suppose we have so filled all these places with romance that there is an unconscious drop in our feelings when we find the people made of clay and the earth composed of sand and loam. Even Westminster Abbey, to which we were driven after our ride, was disappointing, though we found everything we expected to find, and more. I was prepared for the general dinginess of everything about it. It seems to me *sapolio* might improve matters a good deal. Besides, one never feels as he thinks he is going to or as he expects to when standing in a place so full of associations and memories. Not only are there here monuments to the great and good, but there are hosts of hideous, grotesque mortuary emblems, to people long dead and forgotten, that are truly ridiculous. Indeed one sees very few truly fitting memorials of the dead, but huge sarcophagi; and towering, black cenotaphs with designs of most wretched taste. A simple and fitting memorial, one of the most fitting, was that to Sir John Franklin. It was a simple tablet with his bust in relief above, and below a carved representation of a frost and ice bound ship. Below, the words: "O ye frost and O ye snow and ice, praise him," and Tennyson's epitaph:

> "Not here! the white North has thy bones; and thou
> Heroic sailor soul,
> Art passing on thine happier voyage now
> Toward no earthly pole."

Of his wife is said: "She has gone to seek him in higher realms."

At half-past one the Abbey was cleared for the funeral services of General Grant. We had excellent seats in the poet's corner. A more fitting service it would be hard to conceive. The place, the time, the character of the music and the address were all most appropriate. The eulogy of Canon Farrar was such that even I could take no exception to it.   It concerned him as a general, rather than as a man or statesman, and closed with eloquent words upon the oneness of the two nations. Representatives of the Queen and of the Prince of Wales were in attendance, as well as the Duke of Cambridge and Marquis of Lorne.   Chief Justice Waite and Mr. Gladstone were also present.

LONDON, 16 August.

The past ten days have been filled with sightseeing of the most heterogeneous character.   The diary has been as follows:

Wednesday, Aug. 5.—House of Commons; Mme. Tissaud.
Thursday, Aug. 6.—Windsor Castle, Eton, Stoke Pogis.
Friday, Aug. 7.—Tower of London; Shops.
Saturday, Aug. 8.—St. Paul's; Shops.
Sunday, Aug. 9.—Spurgeon.
Monday, Aug. 10.—House of Peers, Westminster Abbey.
Tuesday, Aug. 11.—Inventions, South Kensington.
Wednesday, Aug. 12.—British Gallery.
Thursday, Aug. 13.—Crystal Palace.
Friday, Aug. 14.—Zoological Gardens.

We have found many places of public interest closed to visitors and put under strict police surveillance. This is one of the penalties paid for living in a monarchy. It is very evident that the "dynamite scare" did scare. Such places as the Tower and Parliament House do not open without an open sesame.   Thus we were fortunate to have to this latter place a letter given us by Mr. Howard to Henry Richard, M. P. The Parliament House, vast as it is in extent and tall as are its towers, does not strike one as imposing. It sits too low, directly on the river from which it is seen to the best advantage. It partakes of that same grimy appearance which seems to be a characteristic of all London buildings. It might be four hundred rather than forty years old as far as its appearance goes. I felt inclined to make comparisons unfavorable to it with our own white Capitol. And when inside I did not find myself inclined to yield a point to the British Capitol. Its carvings are in wood and stone rather than in marble. The central hall, octagon in form, bears comparison with our rotunda. But it has no dome. The House of Commons, small, rather plainly furnished, surprised me. I was put in a little cage above the Speaker and at first thought I was in a committee room. It proved to be a day in which every one was airing his peculiar grievance, and we heard several Irish members speak. The manner of speaking seemed to us halting and defective. It was, however, for the most part devoid of attempts at oratory which sometimes make our solons ridiculous. Some of the paintings in the corridors were fine, and all interesting from an historical point of view. It shows the continuity of English history to find pictures of such diverse elements.

Our visit to Windsor proved something of a failure. The day turned rainy before we got home. The place is also perfectly besieged with cabmen and guides and small boys all determined to get their penny or shilling. We were marched through the state apartments in a kind of quick metre time without a chance to ruminate on the immutability of Kings and Empires. Palaces are rather dreary places. They seem more like prisons. St. George's Chapel proved interesting, but into the Albert Chapel we were unable to penetrate (dynamite). This Chapel and the vaults contain the ashes of the family of George III., also those of Henry VIII., Jane Seymour and Charles I. Here the Queen has erected monuments to her father, her aunt, the Duchess of Gloucester and her uncle, King Leopold, "who was to her as a father and to whom she was as a daughter." The monument to the Princess Charlotte is very fine for one with so elaborate a design. It represents the mortal body and the freed spirit. Weeping friends surround the body, angels, one of whom bears her infant, accompany the immortal part.

The stables, be it said, were also interesting, very models of cleanliness. The Queen has only about one hundred and twenty horses. We saw her favorite saddle horse, Jessie, but none of the horses seemed to us wonderfully fine.

Leaving Windsor after dinner we crossed the river to Eton where we wandered about in the various rooms under the conduct of an amiably garrulous old man. He knew us to be Americans and took us into his sanctum where he had a picture of Abbot Lawrence whom he used to know, as well as Daniel Webster and Edward Everett, as he declared. They used to visit his old master. At Stoke Pogis we stood in that little graveyard where the "rude forefathers of the hamlet sleep." Gray himself is buried there, although his monument is in the Park some fifty rods away.

Driving on to Slough in a pouring rain, we took our train, which landed us in due time in London.

Mr. Richard kindly obtained from the war department a pass admitting us to the Tower of London, and thither we bent our steps. A friendly Beefeater (*buffetier*) met us and was the first object of interest, in his costume descended from Henry VIII. It was a blood-curdling place and one thoroughly fitted to fill us with thanksgiving that we live in happier times. The old Norman Chapel (St. John's) of the White Tower is the purest specimen of Roman architecture that we have yet seen. The most pathetic place in England I believe to be the little chapel of St. Peters, where lie buried the many victims of revenge and hate, who have laid down their lives in this unhallowed place,—Anne Boleyn,

Jane Grey, Thomas More, Earl Essex, Lord Guildford Dudley, and many others. It gives one a realizing sense of what it is to live in happier times.

St. Paul's is vast. It did not seem altogether pleasing after the grand Gothic. No other architecture is so fit for the worship of God. When its decorations are complete St. Paul's will be magnificent, but it will not be a church. The monuments seemed to me on the whole less grotesque than those of Westminster Abbey. For the most part they commemorate army and navy officers, prominent among whom are Wellington and Nelson. The whispering gallery, reached by a long staircase, is an amusing example of the echo. The old fuddy-duddy in charge rather hurt the effect.

After St. Paul's we wandered around in Paternoster Row among the book-shops. There are times when it seems we must come upon old Sam. Johnson or stumble upon Steele or Addison. Of all shops the book-shops seem the most unpretending.

The Tabernacle and Spurgeon were the objects of our pilgrimage Sunday morning. An immense audience, in a plain building, were our first impressions. No organ, no choir, the hymns lined off by the minister, who was the one point around which everything revolved. The face of the man was repulsive, but in the sermon there was little to condemn as there was little to praise.

It was devoid of all eloquence, of all fine writing, of all rhetoric, of all illustrations, but was pervaded by the right spirit. This sermon, too, was on the sure foundations: 2 Tim., ii:19. The sermon was evangelistic in the best sense. The congregation was composed of quite ordinary people.

Through Mr. Phelps we obtained a pass for the House of Peers. It was a rare privilege to hear in the course of the hour we were there the Marquis of Salisbury, Earl Eddisleigh, Earl Denman, Earl Milltown, Earl Granville and some others.

We also paid our last visit to Westminster Abbey. On the whole my impression of disappointment does not wear away. We were glad to see the Jerusalem Chamber, a noble room and full of noble memories. The coronation chair was a sorry sight. I suppose English sovereigns will continue to be crowned in it as they have been since the days of Edward the Confessor, but it is well to cover its ugliness with crimson and gold. It is in the retrospect that the Abbey appears to be all that it ought to be, all that it really is. One forgets then all that is incongruous and thinks only of the grand, the pathetic, the sublime.

Wednesday, 12 August.

We gave this day to the National Gallery in Trafalgar Square, and a delightful day it proved. We had an opportunity of studying Turner upon his various sides. In his earlier paintings, which resemble Claude, we find little to admire. But his later pieces are *sui generis*. No other artist has ever attempted to paint, much less succeeded in painting, *motion*. The fire, the whirlwind, the storm under his brush become realities. We had here our first Raphaels,—one recently purchased at a cost of £70,000. We sat before it a long long time waiting to be stirred and moved but we waited in vain. The picture which had the most power over me was Ary Scheffer's St. Augustine and his Mother. Those faces are wonderful. Scheffer excels not in flesh and blood but in soul and spirit. Those calm, intense faces, so like each other in form and purpose, clearly outlined against the cold, grey sky, the sphinx in the distance, live in the memory and I believe always will.

Monday.

We started in the morning to pay our homage at the shrine of that old heathen, Thomas Carlyle. In order to kill two birds we went to London bridge to take a Chelsea boat so that we might have a ride on the river. It was an "experience," and one which I think will serve a life time. London bridge seems to be the aortic valve of London. But as its stream is so impure perhaps it would be better to liken it to the *vena cava*. We wandered about amid all manner of smells, and finally gave a boy a penny to get us on board the boat. The view of the Thames Embankment, of Cleopatra's Needle and the Parliament House repaid us, however. Our good friend Baedeker, which has proved invaluable to us, was left at home and we had to depend on our Yankee tongue. We walked over two miles to find Cheyne Row. This word I had always pronounced in my mind *Sheen*, or the principle of *chicanery*. Mr. Beach called it *Kine* after the analogy of *chiropodist*. Charles split the difference and called it *Chine* like *church*, but when we arrived on the ground the old teamster who gave us our start, called it *Châney*. Such a vaporous thing is fame that we could with difficulty find a man to tell us where dwelt the modern incarnation of selfishness. The shutters were closed and *For Sale* placarded. Charles gazed long down the hole where the returned manuscripts were wont to be deposited. It was a dismal, cheerless place, and it would take much love to make it endurable to any proud and sensitive woman.

The afternoon we made our second attack on the British Museum, but it was almost as futile as the first. I never feel very wise, I often feel very ignorant, but I don't think my ignorance ever has so sensible a weight as when I am in the British Museum.

Tuesday found us wandering amid the delightful fine arts collection of the South Kensington Museum.

It was so cold that I was forced to come home before spending half the time we wished. It is a museum exquisitely arranged and containing beautiful things enough to turn one's head. The afternoon I stayed in for repairs and mended my clothes.

The most delightful day spent in England was that which we passed at Cambridge, Wednesday, August 19th. An express train landed us without a stop upon the banks of the Cam. A hansom drove us at once to Girton. The building is attractive upon first view. Only two stories high, it stretches out wing upon wing catching all possible air and sunshine. If only Vassar buildings could have been erected on such a principle! Everything seemed pleasant and the air of the place was refined and scholarly. The bath-room, bed-room and sitting-room of a suite were cosy and comfortable. The library, a pleasant room, contained a choice though not extensive collection of books. The recitation rooms looked thoroughly feminine in their blue felt rugs and blue table spreads.

Driving back to the city we were left at King's Chapel, that beautiful church for which Cambridge is famed. In it we found it was difficult which to admire more, the stone pillars and arches worked into the most delicate fan tracery in the roof, the wood carvings of the screen or the exquisite windows with their chaste designs and rich colourings. Its general architecture is that of the latest perpendicular Gothic slightly influenced, noticeably in the screen, by the renaissance. From King's Chapel we went to the University library where, through the courtesy of a graduate who happened to be drawing books, we were admitted to the rooms and alcoves. This library, with several others, receives by law a copy of every book copyrighted in the kingdom. It has thus amassed a vast number of books; and it seemed to us like a museum for keeping books rather than a working library. Here, as well as at the British Museum, the cumbrous written catalogue is in vogue. A very small force is employed, only some twelve in all. From the library the same gentleman took us to the Students' Union. Its rooms were handsome. Of course few students are now in the city. Our lunch was followed by a visit to Trinity College. The Chapel, more modern, perhaps more homelike than that of King's College, contained busts and statues of several of Trinity's noble sons: Lord Bacon, Sir Isaac Newton, Dr. Whewell and Macaulay stood out in strongest relief. The library contains row after row of books neatly and tastefully arranged, but like the University library it seems hardly designed for use. Its shelves are open to students as those of the University are not. Here is deposited the telescope of Sir Isaac Newton, and here is the statue of

Byron by Thorwaldson which found a resting place in his
Alma Mater after in vain seeking a place in Westminster. It is a noble work of art. Would the artist had had
a nobler subject ! At Trinity we passed from court to
court, for the colleges are all built about courts, until we
found ourselves by the river. Here an enchanting view
met our eyes;—the broad, low banks of the Cam, crossed
and recrossed by bridges of the most artistic designs; the
rows of trees shading broad walks, the trees fringing the
river and dipping their branches into its waters; the picturesque little boats sculled by stalwart young oarsmen,—all
made the finest picture which we have yet seen in merrie
England. Caught by the spirit of the place we chartered
a row boat and rowed up and down the river past the
colleges until we lighted upon some views not so delightful, when we turned back. In an angle of the great
court at Trinity we found that walk under the chapel
windows where Macaulay wandered back and forth book
in hand, and where Trevellyan says his dim shade must
linger. Every one treated us with great civility, and in the
porter we found a woman who showed us the rooms, close
together, formerly occupied by Macaulay, Newton and
Thackeray.

St. John's College was next visited. We saw its Chapel
and a suite of rooms belonging to rather a gay student
given to entertainments of a non-scholastic sort. Next

we proudly bent our steps to Emanuel College, the fountain of our early Massachusetts culture, the college of
Harvard and Shepard. The porter was just sufficiently
mellowed by the genial influence of the wine cup to be
in a most complaisant mood. To know we were from
Cambridge, New England, was to open the fountain of
his hospitality and knowledge. He favored us with dis-
sertations on the Reformation, with quotations from the
great poets, with dramatic recitations of Shakespere,
with historical reminiscence and college jokes. He took
us to the chapel, where a window memorial to Harvard
tells that his work is not unknown or unappreciated in
his old home. He showed us the rooms which he occupied in college and also the kitchen where the students of the present day draw their good cheer.

At Christ's College we peered through the bars in
vain for a sight of Milton's Mulberry tree. A passing horse
car took us to the station,—and our day in Cambridge
was past. I think our own Harvard seems greater to us
than it did. She may have no King's Chapel, but
neither has Cambridge an Agassiz Museum, a Memorial
Hall or a Hemenway Gymnasium.

Thursday we paid a visit to the Albert Memorial, a
vast and splendid monument erected by Queen Victoria
and her people to the memory of the Prince Consort.
Its cost, £120,000, gives an idea of its magnificence.

The study of its allegorical groups consumed a good deal of our time:—America, represented by a bison and Indian tamed by the hunter, and the goddess of liberty, all satisfied our national pride. The National Portrait Gallery consumed the rest of the day. We found it extremely interesting, containing the portraits of nearly every Englishman and woman of distinction from the days of the Tudors to the present time. Nearly all were by eminent artists and were worth study for their intrinsic merit as well as for their subjects.

Friday was our last day in London and it was with almost homesick feelings that we prepared to leave our comfortable home in Southampton street. Particularly did we linger at the Holborn restaurant where our daily portion of English roast beef has been consumed. We have found living in London very reasonable and very comfortable. The breakfasts are meagre enough and I can't get used to living without fruit. The butter, too, has been a trial. We found considerable packing to do, for, at the last moment, we decided not to take a trunk to the continent. The buying of tickets consumed considerable time, for the stupid Englishman has not yet learned how berths can be secured when tickets are sold at different places.

After dinner we went to the banker's for letters, and thence to the headquarters of the Salvation Army, where we spent a half hour in looking over their literature. It impressed me favorably. It seemed filled with sensible ideas, well calculated to train the class of people among whom it works into principles of truth and duty. The peculiar sensational elements of the system occupied a small part of its pages. An omnibus took us to Trafalgar Square, and thence we began our walk through the Mall to Buckingham Palace, taking Marlborough House, St. James Palace and Clarence House on our right. A strange palace is St. James. Brick stables jumbled together would be almost as beautiful and imposing. Marlborough House we did not find attractive and we took occasion once more, as we have many times before, to bless our stars that we are not royalty.

After a light tea at the Holborn, we were ready for our drive to the Great Eastern Station, where at half-past eight we set out for Harwich. An uneventful ride in company with jolly strangers of several nationalities brought us to the place of embarkation where the Maude Hamilton was waiting to receive us. A comfortable little state-room, or private cabin, as they call it, was reserved for us, and all seemed favorable for a night of calm repose. But, alas, for human calculations! The boat rolled and our stomachs rolled. The kind old stewardess was as sympathetic as could be and full of suggestions. Her prescription for us was champagne which I took with as much alacrity as though I had never been president of a W. C. T. U.! It really allayed the distress, and the rest of the night was passed in uneasy slumber. Charles rebelled against the champagne and it did not seem to have a correspondingly beneficial effect. He preferred to hug his old friend, the brandy bottle.

BRUSSELS, 27 August.

A very busy and very interesting time has been ours. Our eyes have been opened to strange sights and our ears to stranger sounds. We have left Holland with very good opinions regarding our Dutch brothers collectively and individually. A wonderful people is our verdict. They not only cultivate their land and cultivate it highly, but they make the land they cultivate, and rather than fight to win territory, they prefer to encroach upon the domains of old Neptune, and by hard and honest toil to gain their acres. For many of the strange sights we had been prepared by reading and by pictures: the peculiar dress of the working women, in their short petticoats, wooden shoes, caps and gold head-bands; the heavy cart drawn by dogs; the tall, narrow, canting houses; the life,—eating, drinking and talking out of doors. Yet neither pictures nor written descriptions are quite like seeing with one's eyes. The four Dutch towns we were in seemed each to possess some novelty of its own. Rotterdam was peculiar for the number and proportions of its dog teams; Amsterdam for the remarkable tipsy character of its houses, and its system of canals, rivaling those of Venice. At Leyden we saw women, on steps leading to the canals, doing their family washing; at Delft women and dogs were drawing heavy canal boats. How those Dutchmen smoke! It seems to me I did not see a male Hollander without a pipe or cigar. Youngsters of five puff their cigars in company with their elders, and they do not even take out the pipe when they eat. Smoking in restaurants and smoking while eating was a new sight to me. Eating out of doors always had a poetic sound to me, and I had fancied the greensward beneath the feet and the waving branches of the trees above the head. Instead of these delights they set their tables out on the sidewalk, and, blocking the way to pedestrians, quaff their schnapps and puff their pipes. All the towns are kept neat by constant scrubbing, but I could not but think that the centuries of such treatment had rubbed a good deal of dirt in as well as off. Neat and clean the streets certainly are, but an almost entire absence of trees and greensward gives them a bare appearance. The general air of thrift and contentment among the people was striking. Every one whom we saw seemed to be of the common people as we should say, but every one seemed to have some place in life and to be fitted into

it. We saw neither beggars nor quasi-beggars, nor did
any faces bear those dejected, God-forsaken looks which
stamp so many countenances seen on the streets of London.
Nor on the other hand did we see those restless, keen,
driving, sharp cut lineaments so common to the American
faces. The children were plain, but clean, rosy and
happy. The women were hard working, a little dogged
looking perhaps, but strong, as I never saw women
before. It filled me with envy to see them take their
heavy baskets and walk off with such a strong, buoyant
step. It was not perhaps the gait which Mr. Turvey-
drop would strive to impart, but it had the grace of
unconscious strength.

At Rotterdam we did not make a long tarry. Neither
heads nor stomachs were in the best condition to see or
enjoy. We took a carriage for an hour, and accompanied
by a kind of Yankee Dutch boy, who pointed out the
objects of interest in choice Dutch English, rode about
the city. He showed us "Mr. Erasmus" statue and the
house in which he was born; he pointed out to us the
house for "young children who have lost their elders,"
and some other points of interest. At twelve we left for
Amsterdam where a ride of an hour brought us, and
where the Bible Hotel opened to receive us. Our first
pilgrimage was made to the Rijks Museum, a new picture gallery of vast proportions and noble design. I

doubt if any city of the size of Amsterdam can boast a gallery so fine in all respects. The collection of paintings is vast and particularly rich in the works of Dutch artists, chief of whom of course is Rembrandt. Unfortunately the historical character of this museum has introduced a vast number of inferior works.

Sunday morning we started to find the Presbyterian church. By the help of Baedeker and the three languages more or less at our command we expected an easy victory. But we wandered about, and finally found our way in through a back alley where we heard the final words of the discourse. Before going home from church we went to a little gallery which holds the famous picture of Ary Scheffer's, known as Christus Consolator. The picture disappointed us. Like Hamlet, with Hamlet left out, it was Consolator without the Christ. His face expressed but little.

The afternoon was spent in letter writing and in the evening we went out to see the city as it appeared on a Sunday evening. Everyone was out, happy, enjoying himself, yet nothing boisterous or rude. Everything was decorous. It is evident the religious life of the people, as we count religious life, is weak, and Sunday is very little observed. The few Sunday shops were doubtless those of Jews, of whom Amsterdam has a large number.

The oldest city—Leyden—of Holland seemed like an Amsterdam on a small scale. Its University of seven hundred pupils has little to show for itself, since the students have rooms in the town and receive much of their instruction at the houses of the professors. What there was to see we saw, however. In the church of the town rests the body of the great John Robinson, the good John Robinson. In the house close by he lived and worked for many years. It seemed strange, at this little Dutch town, to stand at the grave of one, who, without ever being in New England, influenced so potently New England life and character. We fancied that the Pilgrims did not leave Holland entirely free from the influence of their Dutch neighbors. A certain ugliness in the churches seemed strangely familiar.

We reached the Hague in the first of the afternoon and soon made our way to the picture gallery. Here we found the most wonderful of Rembrandt's pictures which we have yet seen, An Anatomical Lecture. The triumph of life over death is most remarkable. There, too, is Paul Potter's famous Bull,—a wonderful animal, but hardly so wonderful to us as to his masters. This gallery was choice, nearly every picture having merit of its own.

The Binnenhof, a low, irregular brick structure, ancient and hoary, which served for Parliament House and government offices, next claimed our attention. The rooms of state were somewhat fine, and that fitted up with a certain magnificence by William III. was of special interest, because in it the articles of the treaty of Ryswick were agreed upon. In trying to find the chambers of the States General we invaded a doughty Dutchman in his lair and were ignominiously shown the way out. Some way royalty appears very cheap in Holland in comparison with England. No red-coated soldiers with bushy hats and bristling bayonets guard these precincts, and no notices even are posted that "packages are not admitted." The palace, which we saw from the outside, is a plain cream-colored building without great pretensions. These Dutch are thrifty fellows and do not mean to squander much on Kings.

A pleasant little variety was added to our day by an evening trip to Scheveningen, a fashionable watering-place. With the setting sun and rising moon and the music and crowds of gaily dressed people, the scene was very picturesque and attractive. It reminded me of a picture in the Corcoran Art Gallery, at Washington, which I think must delineate this place. The wicker booth chairs were a new and pretty feature of seaside life.

Tuesday morning we visited Delft, not the Delfshaven of the Pilgrims. Like Amsterdam and Leyden it seemed a busy, work-a-day town. The Hague has not so much this appearance. The monument to the Prince of Orange, over his grave in the Nieuwe Kerk, and the Prinsenhof, where he was killed, were the chief points of interest. Brave, true, patriotic man, it was a joy to stand upon his grave and pay homage to his memory. Few grander things are in history than his order to pierce the dykes. The figures of justice, prudence, religion, liberty, upon his monument seemed wonderfully fitted to express his character. It was on the canals between The Hague and Delft that we saw the women drawing canal boats. The house where Spinoza lived and a statue recently erected to him claimed our attention on our walk home after leaving the car.

On our arrival at Antwerp we found that, owing to the International Exposition, the city was much crowded, and at one time we feared lest we should not be able to find a bed. A modest little house, Hotel Holland, clean and neat, however, finally opened its doors to us. Mine host proved a genial fellow, and on the whole we did not regret the necessity which brought us to his doors. The day was too far spent for much sight seeing, but in the evening we rode to the Exposition, which resembled all other expositions. The exhibit of lace so fascinated me, however, that I could have lingered hours by it.

The early morning found us on our way to the Museum of Pictures. The walk along the beautiful docks, built and maintained at great expense, was interesting. We see signs of being in another country, although the Dutch and Flemish element seems to predominate. Yet French is the language spoken, and in that tongue we made our way about. I found my vernacular French a good deal rusted after its ten years of disuse, but it is coming rapidly back. Railroad nomenclature I never learned, and the necessary inquiries at the stations are proving puzzling.

At the Antwerp Museum we had an opportunity to study Rubens at his best. The life, the action, of Rubens' masterpieces are wonderful. In these remarkable qualities we have seen no picture to compare with the Crucifixion in the Antwerp Gallery. The figures are few, and each expresses intense activity, all bending to a unity of purpose. Here was not the Mater Dolorosa, but the Mater Dolens, not the sorrowful but the sorrowing mother. It was the first of Rubens' masterpieces which we saw, and may have so filled us that we have no room left properly to estimate the others. But certain it is, that the Descent from the Cross, which we studied long at the Cathedral, will not linger in our minds as will the Crucifixion. Van Dyke's treatment of the Crucifixion and Entombment seemed a bit cold beside Rubens'. I often wonder why so many great artists choose to delineate the horrible, particularly as connected with

religion.   I was fairly sickened by the pictures of horrors which the Museum presented, and felt that our
Blessed Lord had been blasphemed in the execrable
paintings in which profane hands had delineated his suf-
ferings.   We are now in a Catholic country, and do not
fail to see it.

From the Museum we turned toward the Exposition,
to see the exhibition of Beaux Arts.   It is something of an
education simply to wander through these long-galleries
and to look at the wonderful productions of man's skill.
It was interesting also to compare the styles of art of the
different countries.   In none was striking originality
manifest.   The French style of half tints predominated
in the greater part of the paintings.   Modern art seems
to me as perfect in its execution, as exact a representative of nature in form and coloring as the ancient, but it
satisfies itself with too trivial subjects, and fails to move
because failing to present any great thought or feeling.
A picture, like a sermon or poem, must have a subject
which, independent of its execution, will move and in-
spire.   The Russian exhibit interested us, and seemed to
possess power and originality.   One picture in the Belgian
exhibit (The Last Day of Pompeii) and one in the Austrian (The Condemnation of Mars) live with us.

The church at Antwerp (Notre Dame) presented no
striking features in architecture, and was of interest

chiefly because of Rubens' masterpieces which I have before alluded to. It was our first Catholic church, and was filled with images, altars, pictures and trappings to which we are unaccustomed. They seemed so cheap and tawdry, often so revolting. I trust they serve to draw some souls nearer our Blessed Lord.

From Antwerp, which we left at five fifty-six, to Brussels, we traveled in a most uncomfortable car, half American, half English, losing the comforts of each. Smoking was indulged, and I had to breathe it in. Oh, if it were only true that smoking breeds cancers!

BRUSSELS, 27 August.

In Belgium's capital! And it seems as if even now were gathered here a kingdom's beauty and chivalry. Such a different city from the work-a-day Dutch towns! Youth and pleasure here seem to meet, and on every side are pleasure's ministers. Art and nature, the beautiful in form, in architecture, all are here to delight the eyes. The drives are full, the parks are full, and the workers only seem to work to minister to the seeker of beauty and pleasure. The windows are full of laces, of gems, of painting, to tempt the beholder. The squares and parks are adorned with flowers and statues to Belgian heroes. The Palais de Justice is one of the most remarkable specimens of modern architecture. Like our own beautiful Capitol, it rises upon a slight eminence at the end of one of the principal avenues of the city. It is so magnificent as almost to satiate. Down in the valley is the Hotel de Ville, a fine Gothic building of the fourteenth century, and a grand specimen of the secular art which flourished in the Netherlands, and of which England has hardly a trace. The Square of the Petit Sablon is a delightful little spot. A little garden in which stands a statue of Counts Egmont and Hoorn, on their way to execution, is surrounded by a paling on the pilasters of which are small brazen statues representing the trades of Belgium. The boulevards are broad, forming a complete circuit of the city. Everything is French.

In going to Waterloo we took the steam train to Braine l'Alleud, and thence an omnibus to the center of the field. The two hours on the field allowed us to visit but few of the spots of interest, but with our guide and books the short time was enough to gain an excellent idea of the proceedings of that awful day. Pray God such scenes may never be repeated on the green earth that He has made! Nothing seems to me so monstrous as war, and it is a constant marvel that it has survived eighteen Christian centuries. We saw some sights on our ride to the battle field strange to our American eyes. Little children followed our *bus* for a mile begging for pennies. The women were hoeing and raking in the fields, and one we

saw shoveling manure.   After dinner we went out walking, and found much to enjoy in the beautiful city.

Friday morning we went out lace hunting.   It was
a wonder we did not spend all our money on the fascinating stuff.   We bought all our consciences would allow,
and yearned for less Puritan consciences.   It was hard
for me even to turn my steps to the Museum of Paintings,
and I found that among its treasures my busy mind re-
verted to the fabrics of loveliness that my eyes had seen.
This gallery is rich in specimens of every type of Flemish art.   Two pictures by Thomas, Judas and Barabbas,
struck us as original in conception and powerful in execution.   Gallait's Abdication of Charles V. was a fine
picture, yet open to some criticism.   Early art does not
interest me, still Van Eyck's Adam and Eve were interesting.   The Hotel de Ville received a flying visit.   The
tapestries were the best we have yet seen.   One of the
large salles, we were told, was the place of the ball given
by the Duchess of Richmond on the eve of Waterloo.
This I think is a mistake. We took a carriage to the Place
of Martyrs, thence round the Cathedral to the Palace of
Nations or the Capitol, as we should say.   The legislative
hall of the upper chamber is a gem.   Exquisite carvings
and the portraits of all the Belgian monarchs from Charlemagne to Leopold, by Gallait, noble works of art,
adorn it. The various committee rooms, foreign relations,

etc., were arranged and decorated with great taste and elegance. A dinner, an evening walk finished the day, and it was with real regret that we made our preparations for leaving Brussels and the Netherlands. Particularly did we regret to part with the friendly porter of the Hotel de France, whose kindly smile sped us on our way and welcomed us back from our wanderings. The European porter is an institution, a universal genius, who knows everything and can talk all languages, and is always ready for a fee. It hurt my feelings to give so learned and urbane an individual a paltry franc. We are glad to go to hotels where English is spoken. I find it quite a little strain to carry on negotiations in French, with the possibilities of not always understanding and being understood. But my French has been a good deal brushed up for two days' wear, and by the time I get to Paris I hope to become quite fluent. Going from French to German is a little confusing.

Saturday morning, at nine-forty, we left for Cologne, which, with a stop of two hours at Aix la Chapelle, proved a day's journey. The journey we rather enjoyed. It was restful, and gave us some opportunities for reading and seeing the country and people. The only reason for stopping at Aix was to visit the church built by Charlemagne, where he was buried, and where for eight hundred years after him the German Emperors were crowned. Here for the first time we met Catholic superstition. We paid three marks for viewing relics, some of them intrinsically interesting for their richness, but more sad and revolting. I could bear a link of St. Peter's chain, or a tooth of St. Thomas, but when a man pretends to show me a bit of the shroud of our Lord, and the rope which tied His blessed body to the cross, I shrink and tremble with the horror of the desecration. The marble chair of the Emperors, I presume, is veritable. It may also be that we saw the leg bone of Charlemagne, since his body was disinterred within historic times. But one could but feel suspicious. The architecture of the building was as interesting as the relics.

In Aix la Chapelle, or Aachen, we were in Germany. The burly custom officer who examined our baggage, or, rather, did not examine it, was German. The ticket examiner, who nearly frightened me out of my wits, was also German. The men who smoked in the waiting room were German, all were German. *I don't like them.*

The smells of Cologne did not strike us all at once. The first we detected were in our room, which we tried to analyze in vain, but finally we referred them to the soap with which the bedding was washed. And such a bed! Feather bed beneath, feather bed above, the whole mountain high. It did not look attractive. Sunday

morning we discovered other smells. Surface draining
and sausage were the principal ones.

Sundays spent in traveling are not what Sundays ought
to be, and a Sunday in Germany is quite different from a
Sunday in England. Shops are open, streets are full,
and all is gayety, even to card-playing. It was very
pleasant to find our way into a bit of an English chapel,
very pleasant to join in the "God Lord deliver us" of the
Litany. From so many things have we need to be
delivered! The clergyman read the service slowly with
a strong German accent, and never has it seemed more
impressive. From this service we went to the Cathedral.
It reached our expectation. Grand, vast, almost misty
in its distances, it stretches up and away, a very Gloria in
Excelsis in stone. In it we were also treated to more
relics, the last I think I shall give a sou for seeing.
The rest of the day I passed in my room. We find ourselves comfortable and have, so far, liked the German
table better than the English. The waiter here is most
agreeable and astonished us beyond measure by greeting
us with "holloa" upon going to breakfast. That is
English as she is spoke in Germany.

GENEVA, 6 September.

A week of rapid travel finds us for our Sabbath in
this city of Calvin. In it we have seen few of the

wonders of man's making, but our eyes have been filled with the glories of God's universe. Monday was our day on the Rhine. We went on board the little steamer at seven and left it late in the afternoon at St. Goar for the train, which brought us to Mayence. As far as Bonn the sail was uninteresting; from Bonn to Coblentz it compared very well with Dead River. But between Coblentz and St. Goar its crags and peaks, its castles and vine-clad hills, justified its renown. I began to feel my ignorance of history. To the German, its banks and castles are as full of poetry, romance and chivalry as the banks of the Dee or the crags of Scotland.

The city of Worms, made famous by the brave position of Luther, is not unmindful of the lustre shed upon itself by the great reformer. A bronze statue, or rather monument, of elegant design and strong and vigorous execution is raised to his memory in one of the principal squares of the town. The house no longer stands where met the famous Diet, but to the spot, now occupied by a fine private residence, we made a pilgrimage. Charles walked about the town, which had only such interest as a foreign town always possesses in the eyes of a stranger. While I waited for him in a picture store I listened to a vigorous dispute between three or four young men upon some political matter. It was the day before the anniversary of Sedan and the military spirit was aroused. All these young fellows spoke English well. It is really mortifying to find how well these Germans speak English. Our country is most unfavorably situated for acquiring a foreign tongue.

We continued our journey to Strassburg, where we had all too short a time to inspect the glories of the Cathedral and the interests of the city. I should have been glad to drive about the fortifications of the town, which are in the most perfect style of modern warfare. It is said that every vestige of that cruel siege has disappeared, but the scenes were very fresh to me in both memory and imagination. I had just been reading the Memoir and Letters of the Princess Alice and I could but reflect that the agony she endured and which her letters describe, was no more than that of every wife and mother whose dear ones were enlisted on either losing or winning side. How I hate war ! More and more are its pomp and circumstance distasteful. Germany, I can see, is hardly more than a vast arsenal. Troops are recruited and drilled much as they were with us during the years '61–'65. We saw, at Cologne, a thousand men marching to drill. At Mayence are stationed eight thousand men, at Metz fourteen thousand. Almost equal to our whole army! The Cathedral at Strassburg was a surprise. The wonders of its clock have been allowed to eclipse the glories of its architecture. It is singularly beautiful. Its stone, a reddish brown, was a pleasing relief to the stone-grey in which all the Cathedrals we have before seen, have been built. Its decoration without is peculiarly rich and delicate. A statue of Gutenberg, and the house where the first printing was done, completed the wonders which our limited time allowed us to see. It was eleven o'clock when we reached Basle and we were too tired and sleepy to be very critical of the accommodations offered by The Crown. Our beds were clean, and that is the first thing. The river Rhine, directly in front of the house, went rushing, roaring by, as if just let loose from its mountain home. Before going to the station we rode for a half an hour about the town. It is essentially a German city.

We arrived in Berne a little after one o'clock and at once took a carriage for a quick inspection of the city. We drove to the banker's for letters, but as he was out we took our ride first. The city is beautifully situated upon the banks of the lake and built upon an abrupt height. The distant Alps are in full view, and in winding about among the tortuous narrow streets one constantly finds glorious views bursting upon himself. We had our first view of the Alps from the cars. Like clear blocks of solid, polished quartz they towered into heaven far above the clouds. The Cathedral, Protestant Calvinistic, was inferior in beauty and interest to most buildings bearing

the name.   The city itself we found picturesque, reminding us in some ways of Edinburgh.   The buildings
of some of the old streets were not unlike the rows of
Chester.   The second story, however, was built out over
the sidewalk and was not a second story of street.   Our
driver, who was anxious to make the time as long as
possible, insisted upon taking us across the river to the
bear gardens.   These pits were very large and of stone,
quite eclipsing those of the London Zoo.   Only two of
the six bruins consented to appear.   Our last visitation at
Berne was made to the Bundes Rath House (the Capitol).
It was a building simple in adornment, but well fitted for
its purpose.   From the roof we had a magnificent view of
the city and distant Alps.

The half past six train brought us to Interlaken
about ten.   The sail across Lake Thun in the solemn
stillness of the night, under the shadows of the towering
mountain, was soothing to soul and body.   It is strange
to me that foul deeds stalk abroad at night.   Then, to me,
is conscience most keenly awake, passion most still, and
God most near.   This sail and the sail down the Rhine
were very rich in reminiscences of by-gone times.   In my
mind the German ballads learned so long ago, some
almost forgotten, came to life again.   The old college
days and the old college friends seemed nearer than for
years.   Lines of German poetry, scenes of Wilhelm Tell,

came trooping up and made the rocks and hills peopled and alive.

Interlaken seems all hotels and fancy shops. The *Jungfrau* received us. The morning light revealed to us the beauty of our situation. Directly in front, bathed with the morning radiance, towered the massive whiteness of the hoary Jungfrau. How it glistened and gleamed in the light, an opal in emerald setting! We were impatient of breakfast and eager to be away. The air was intoxicating, like the air of our native mountains, and, but for the snowy, distant summits, we could well imagine ourselves in the mountains of Maine. In the Jungfrau we thought we detected a resemblance in form to Old Blue. We had not walked long before we found the glories of nature eclipsed by the glories of the shops. Swiss carvings proved too great an attraction, and before we left the shop we had well-nigh emptied our purses. The bears, too, were fascinating; carved bears in every variety of size and occupation.

We engaged an amiable charioteer and a somewhat dilapitated chariot to take us to Lauterbrunnen, and the ride was one never to be forgotten. As we wound about among the mountains, the more distant silver-covered summits seemed to play hide and seek with the green heights of the nearer mountains. The castellated crags springing like titan pillars a thousand feet toward the sky; the rushing gray-green waters of the glacial river; the green pastures and picturesque chalets; the clear sky and the fresh air, all seemed like the wonders of the promised land. The little village at Lauterbrunnen, a mere straggling row of houses, offered many tempting objects to our views. Outside the women sat making lace, and the men carving stone figures. It was strange to find, in one house, that German only was spoken, while at the next, French was alone understood.

A pretty walk of half an hour led us to the Staubbach which leaps hundreds of feet off the rocky mountain side to the meadow below. It was late in the afternoon when we returned to Interlaken, and writing letters and dinner brought us to the setting sun. Walks and inspection of the shop-windows con-sumed the evening.

The journey to Geneva occupied all of Friday. We retraced our way to Berne and by rail to Lausanne. At that point our plan had been to take the boat across the lake, but the rain of the day prevented and we finished our journey by rail. The views were fine, and the bursting of the clouds and the succession of showers, followed by a rainbow, diversified the landscape, which in itself was wonderfully beautiful. Yet when the distant Alps are out of view, it would not be hard to fancy myself at home, so similar are the veiws. There is, however, a peculiar abruptness to these mountains. They do not seem to have been finished up and polished off as carefully as ours. The lights and shadows, as they play upon the hillsides and valleys, are wonderful.

At first Geneva did not strike me pleasantly, but its charms gradually grew upon me. All Saturday morning we climbed up and down its steep and narrow streets, and wound in and out their tortuous ways. To many it seemed difficult to find either entrance or exit. Every few minutes one is brought up against some high wall, and on searching for an egress finds it a dark and winding stairway, or through some archway enters into a broad place. The Cathedral, the Museum, the University were the points of public interest which we saw.

In the afternoon we had an experience. We took the omnibus for Fernex, a small suburb over the boundary of France, and which was founded by Voltaire. The omnibus was filled with market women returning home, and very merry was the clatter of the tongues. It gave us a touch of real life. Yet that is not wanting. So much of the life here is out of doors. The streets are filled with women selling their produce, and filling their water jars at the public fountains which abound. At Berne we saw women doing their washing at the basins in the streets, and here we see what seem to be public lavatories, where women bring their clothes and wash in the running water.

The chateau, built by Voltaire, still stands, and is a charming country place. From the terrace a fine view is gained. Two of the rooms remain as he left them, his parlor and sleeping room. In the parlor is a tomb, where the heart of the great scoffer is buried. We left with a kindlier feeling for this prince of sceptics, after seeing the church he built for the people of Fernex.

A Sunday at Geneva and in the house of Calvin is hardly kept with Puritanical strictness. On our way to church we met people evidently off for picnics, and the marching and band-playing were not like Sunday. Yet most shops are closed and the streets decorous. We found a little American Episcopal chapel, where we worshiped with some eighty others. It was a blessed privilege to receive the sacrament in this foreign land. The same God, the same Savior, the same faith.

LUCERNE, 12 September.

A seven o'clock start upon Monday morning, 5th September, brought us to Chamounix at a little before four. The morning was glorious and we took our seats in the diligence with full expectation of a fine day. But the fiend was there, six fiends were there, and by a strange co-incidence, or rather fatality, they all sat in front of me. It was awful. One fiend, with a one-eyed glass, smoked two pipes and five cigars, besides drinking two bottles of wine at dinner. A party of Americans occupied the seats with us. They had a courier; and of all insufferable, impertinent appendages, a courier seems the worst. Think of his puffing a cigar into the ladies' faces! The views, however, were fine. The immense, towering crags and overhanging rocks, as well as the distant mountains, formed a wilder and bolder scene than any we had seen; but while at dinner at Sallanches a hard rain set in, which neither ceased nor lessened until we were in Chamounix. Henceforth we were in a box filled with that vile smoke. I became thoroughly sickened and poisoned.

In the hard, cold rain there seemed little to do but to be comfortable. A fire in the reading room of the Angleterre aided us in this endeavor. From the window we could occasionally catch in the rift of the clouds a view of the monarch mountain, at whose base we were.

The morning of Tuesday seemed little propitious for Alpine climbing. Clouds gathered and let fall a few drops of rain and then parted to show us the sun. It was the opinion of wiseacres that by eleven all would be clear. A little before ten we thought it wise to venture up Montanvert to the "Mer de Glace." We accordingly ordered a guide and a mule for myself, Charles walking. My position on the back of the mule seemed somewhat precarious, and it was only the knowledge that what had been done could be done, which kept me on while the animal toiled over perpendicular precipices. I had an idea that mules were given to kicking and I was possessed of a subdued terror lest Rossa employ his heels in a surreptitious manner, and the problem of where I should land occupied my leisure moments. The guide was very friendly, and kept up a constant stream of conversation, all in French, to which I replied as best I could during the titillations of Rossa. Half way up we stopped at what they call a chalet. I never knew before just what a chalet is. Our word *shanty* is derived from it, I judge! Here we had the pleasure of gazing upon a chamois which we had supposed to be a goat, until we were requested to leave 20 centimes for having looked at him. On we pushed, the guide giving us all kinds of inducements to cross the Mer de Glace, an expedition against which I was firmly set. But gradually I yielded. The longer I sat on Rossa's back the more delightful seemed the prospect of climbing fields of ice upon my feet. An inspection of the Mer from the hotel at Montanvert deepened the desire, and after a little rest and luncheon we started, I and the guide ahead, Charles following. The ice fields disappointed me. I had pictured a glacier as a huge extent of rock candy. It resembles mere dirty snow. Yet in some of the crevasses was seen that peculiar blue tint never seen in anything else, unless it might be in a huge chrysoprase. Once across, the worst was begun. Over rocks and streams and down precipices in steps cut in solid rock, made slippery by rain, we went. We fixed our eyes on a distant white rock, and measured with our eyes every inch which our steps lessened. At last the chateau and a shelter from the rain, which had been for some time falling! Fifteen minutes more of easier climbing, and we see Rossa's ears erect, immovable. The going down was worse than the coming up. Could I keep on? The distance over his head was short, but Rossa was sure-footed, and soon we were in the highway. The rain poured, but it hurt us not. Before six we were in our rooms, our clothes off and dressed again for supper.

At ten o'clock of Wednesday we started in a private carriage for Martigny. The said private carriage seemed to have been built with the special idea of racking every bone and muscle made susceptible by Rossa. The first part of the way over a new military road was smooth, but there followed two miles, in process of making, which were intolerable. The road wound in loops back and forth, up the mountain side, past the glacier Argentière, more beautiful than the Mer de Glace, over rushing, roaring torrents, and along the edges of precipices to the Bete Noire House, in the Bete Noire pass. Here we arrived at one o'clock for dinner, and here the horses, which had hardly left a walk and had come barely three miles an hour, found it necessary ''to repose,'' as the coachman said. All day long the sun had played hide and seek, and now the rain began in earnest and hardly abated until we reached, somewhat sore and stiff, the Hotel du Mont Blanc, at Martigny. All through the country by which we came were scattered those miserable little houses, usually in groups, which seemed the abodes of want, dirt and ignorance. Never have I seen civilized people who impressed me as so low in the scale of being as these Swiss peasants. Pitiably poor was everything about them. The women in the woods breaking off dry twigs and branches, and carrying them home in loads upon their backs ; the low, miserable huts, which on one side served as house and on the other as stable, or, worse yet, stable below and house above, seemed wretched beyond description. Yet no village was without its chapel, no turn in the road without its cross.

The ride in the steamer from Bouveret to Ouchy, over the east end of Lake Léman, was grand yet calming. The sun was setting and lighted every part of the landscape with that radiance only seen at sunset. The Dent du Midi stood up boldly, snow-capped and sun-tipped. The bright little watering places, Vevay among them, and the Castle of Chillon, all were full of beauty and poetry, the poetry of life and the poetry of imagination.

Ouchy was delightful. At breakfast we watched the white-capped waves of blue as they dashed against the wharves. Apparently they came in with great fury, for the spray was thrown at times twenty feet in air.

Friday, September 11th, we spent in the cars. From Ouchy to Lausanne is a ride of less than a mile in a *bus*. The day proved rainy, a fact that showed the wisdom of our decision in regard to the Furka pass. We reached Lucerne at four twenty-five, and found a home at St. Gotthard's near the station. After tea a walk in the mist showed us but little of the beauties of the town, and the most of the evening we spent in writing. The town, however, is most beautiful for situation. Upon a bend in the lake, it sweeps about it in a crescent form, and embraces in its extent the beauties of the distant mountains, rising range after range until the snow-capped summits blend in the sky. On one side the Rigi, on the other the Pilatus stand as sentinels. The Pilatus, in its rugged grandeur, surpasses any mountain I have seen.

Saturday morning we decided to attempt the Rigi, although the day was unpropitious. No rain actually fell, but snow had fallen upon the top of the mountain, and that reduced to slush made going about quite impossible. But the ride upon the lake and also on the railway disclosed beautiful views. To me, however, the Lion of Lucerne was the attraction of the town. Three pilgrimages I made to his solitary resting place, and was each time awed by his pathetic grandeur. No such fitting monument, I am sure, has ever been raised to human heroism. There the wounded lion rests in a niche in the rock of the eternal mountains, the calm water at his feet, the dark woods about him, one paw limp and lifeless, but the other, with the tenacity of a death struggle, grasps the lilies of France. I shall always remember the picture.

A walk about the town revealed a lack of the gayety and life of the quays and hotels,—a dense German population.

On Sunday we found our way to the English church, a somewhat pretentious yet fitting house of worship. As usual the sermon was of a low order, but the service was, as always, enjoyable. Few things so impress upon me the oneness of all Christian people as the worship in the English church of a Continental town. It was an inspiration to sing "Onward Christian Soldier," by the Lake of Lucerne, blending our voices with hundreds of men and women, all of different lands and nations.

An early start was necessary on Monday morning in order that we might sleep in Heidelberg. The journey, made a part of the way in a fast train, was delightful. From Basle, where we changed cars, we had the company of an English gentleman, a Colonel in the army, and his wife. He proved a sociable and interesting companion. The great interest of the day proved to be the ride through the Black Forest, where the cars make a descent of nineteen hundred feet in twenty-five miles. We wound around and down, sometimes seeing the track over which we were to pass hundreds of feet below us; sometimes seeing that over which we had come quite as far above. No less than thirty-eight tunnels of different lengths were passed through. At Carlsruhe an American gentleman and lady, from California, entered our carriage. They were bright and pleasant, and we found them again at our hotel at Heidelberg. The man presented the phenomenon of a man without a language. Born in Cuba, he lived there until some eight years old, and then was at school in France some five years. He then went to Heidelberg, where he remained until about twenty, and then went to the United States, where his last ten years have been passed. He spoke English with a marked German accent.

The Hotel de l'Europe opened hospitable doors to us at Heidelberg. It was already past eight when we arrived, and bed was the only attraction. But early in the morning we began our explorations of the town. For the casual visitor it presents little besides the University and the Schloss. It is, of course, vacation in the university, and the principal building in the center of the town is undergoing repairs. I did not go in, but Charles moved round among the rooms and library. It was necessary to take a carriage for the Castle, nine hundred feet above the level of the town. We drove first to the heights above, where we could look down upon the ruins below, magnificent even in ruins. The Castle, in its days of glory, must have formed a city in itself. Belonging to a later day than any of the ruined castles of England, it presents many beauties of architecture. The Otto Heinrich's castle is a remarkably fine specimen of Renaissance architecture. Alas, my knowledge of German history proves sadly inadequate for the proper appreciation of these castles.

The day proved uncomfortably warm, and after leaving the carriage we really found the heat oppressive. It was our wish to see the room where the students fight their duels, and for this purpose we were obliged to cross the Neckar. In the upper chamber of a modest guest-house, known as the *Hirsch*, the silly boys hack at each other. We met one of the idiots with a dozen or more gashes in his face. We found our way back to the hotel, and, taking a simple dinner, left at four o'clock for Frankfort.

Frankfort pleased us because, in its newer parts, it resembles an American city. Our walk in the early evening was very pleasant. Our hotel, the Swan—somewhat famous as being the place where the Treaty of Frankfort, at the close of the Franco-Prussian war, was signed—was near many points of interest. The monuments of Schiller, Goethe and Gutenberg are impressive. We took the horse cars a little before eight, and soon found ourselves in a real German beer garden. It was indeed a beautiful spot. Lighted by hundreds of jets, the water, the grass, the trees, the flowers, all looked like fairy land. The flowers were very fine. Great beds of calladiums, of cannas, of hydrangas, of coleas, of salvias, of every beautiful foliage or flowering plant, were arranged in charming taste. The house, the former palace of a Prince of Nassau, was converted into refreshment rooms. But the music was the chief attraction. It was of a light order, Strauss and the like, but beautifully rendered with string instruments.

Charles sat up late arranging a perfect plan for sight-seeing which would enable us to take the twelve-forty train for Weimar. He succeeded admirably. We left the house promptly at eight, and proceeded to the Panorama to see a painting of the Battle of Sedan. Upon arrival we found that an enterprising Yankee had transported the picture to America, and a painting of the first battle of the war, Weissenburg, had taken its place. It simply served to deepen our horror of war. From the Panorama we turned to Bethmann's Museum, a small private collection, containing Dannecker's Ariadne on the Panther. This work of the Stuttgart artist, of the first of the present century, is worthy to be placed side by side with the work of the great Greek sculptors. Indeed, I hardly know what work equals it in the poise and litheness of the figure. It is shown under a light which both conceals certain defects in the marble and throws a life-like appearance upon it. Next in order came, in the Römer, the Kaisersaal. This building faces a mediæval square quite in contrast with the new parts of the city. The point of interest is the Hall of the Emperors, which contains portraits of the Emperors from Charlemagne to Charles V. and his obscure successors. The house in which Goethe was born is kept as a memorial, and shows clearly the easy circumstances of his family. The memorials of the poet, consisting of pictures taken at various times, pages of Wilhelm Meister, his writing desk, lock of hair, etc., all served to bring him nearer to us.

The ride of a little more than seven hours to Weimar in a fast train was very pleasant but brought to us nothing of special interest.

The Russischer Hof at Weimar welcomed us. We did not find it luxurious, but it was comfortable. All the hotels we have so far found on the continent give us fresh, clean beds. We were glad to be at rest after a busy day. But the next day, Thursday, was destined to be busier yet. Weimar seemed full of interest. It is the capitol of Saxe-Weimar as well as the literary center of the olden time. The statue of the Dichter-Paar, Goethe and Schiller, was the first point of interest. A most fine and fitting memorial, too, it is. Near by is the house where Schiller lived, worked, and died. The rooms are still shown. The bed on which he died, decked with wreathes, is pointed out. We found his grave as well as that of Goethe in what the Germans so beautifully call the Friedhof, and in the tomb of the Grand Duke they both sleep together.

Herder and Wieland have statues at Weimar. Like all the bronze figures we have seen in Germany, they are excellent. Time forbade us to visit the Schloss or the Kirche, in both of which are fine paintings. But we wanted to crowd Jena with its university into the day, and yet sleep at Leipsic. This we were able to do by taking a train before noon, for Jena lies but an hour away. In Jena, being a small town somewhat off from the line of travel, we found no English spoken, but summoning all our reserve force we met our occasion and conquered. A bust of Schiller by Dannecker, placed on the spot where he composed Wallenstein when a professor at the university, interested me, but the university I allowed Charles to visit alone.

In getting to the Denkmal we were obliged to go through
a professor's house and passed the family at their dinner
on a kind of back piazza.   It looked cosy.

We fulfilled our plans and slept in Leipsic at the
Hotel Hauffe.   Friday morning I felt quite willing that
Charles should investigate the problem of university
education at Leipsic, alone.   Leipsic seemed to offer few
attractions.   It is a great commercial town.   We therefore decided to spend the remainder of the day at Halle
and go thence to Wittenberg for the night.   A ride of an
hour about town enabled us to see the Rosenthal park,
as well as many of the streets.   The theatre is a fine
building of the Greek order.   The trip to Halle began
inauspiciously.   I was unfortunate enough to address a
soldier as a railroad official and a university student as a
horse car conductor, and their inward wrath showed
outwardly and was overpowering.   We were able to find
our way about very well, however.   Charles went into
several buildings of the university, and we both went to
the new library, a fine brick building, holding three
hundred thousand volumes, erected in 1880.   It seemed
to be admirably arranged for work.

It was quite late when we arrived at Wittenberg.
Die Goldene Weintraube did not seem over-attractive.
A friendly word in our native tongue greeted us, but a
huge hogshead had to be passed in the hall.   Our room

was very comfortable, and we suffered no inconvenience on account of speaking German. Our Baedeker played us false, but fortunately we found a map in the office and devoted our evening to planning the next day. The morning light showed us a quaint old town with little sign of change since Luther trod the streets. In front of the hotel in the Market place were gathered the usual crowd of women with all kinds of produce for sale, a sight common on market days in all German towns. When it began to rain it seemed not to affect anyone. For those who had booths or umbrellas, it was well. For those who had not, it was all the same. In this market stand two bronze statues, one of Luther and one of Melanchthon, which are in no way wonderful. The Luther oak, which marks the spot where Luther burned the papal bull, we piously sought. Our matter of fact guide-book swept away all feeling of sentiment by telling us that this place was not the real place, only erroneously supposed to be. Be that as it may, no doubt exists but that his home was in the old Augustinian, a monastery, now used as a theological seminary. In these rooms are many memorials of him; the table where he wrote, the pulpit from which he preached, the curious double chair in which he and his wife sat (a thoroughly German affair, his side with a back, hers with none), pictures of himself, pages of his manuscript, collections of his books, and, carefully cherished, his beer-mug which, to do him justice, was smaller than most of those one sees in Germany.

Standing upon such spots one can never feel as he ought to feel, yet I think I had a deep feeling of awe in the old Stadt Kirche, where for the first time the blood of our Lord was drunk in the fruit of the wine. It means so much to us all that that man dared. I wanted, too, to see the prints of the nails in the door of the old Schloss Kirche, but the door no longer stands. Its lineal successor was also covered while repairs on the church were in progress. Here is his grave, and near by that of his friend Melanchthon. Other men might have done his work, but he did it. Pious ones will ever turn their steps toward Wittenberg.

At one o'clock we were en route for Berlin, and arrived in time to get our mail at the banker's, which made our heart light by good news all around from home. We found pleasant quarters reserved for us by Frau Fulleborn, 44 Jerusalem Strasse. It was a change and a relief to sit down to a table filled with pleasant people, all Americans except the family. We were prepared to rest to the full extent of the Fourth Commandment. Sunday morning we found a little American Chapel, where we heard an excellent sermon, a sermon really refreshing. There is a strong tendency to let down the tone of our spiritual life when away from all associations, and the sermons we have heard since coming to the Continent are not of a type to stir deeply the spiritual life. We spoke with the clergyman after service and found him to be Professor Stuckenberg. Part of the afternoon a young New Yorker, a student, *Mr. Armstrong by name, spent in our room, and part we spent in writing.

Monday morning we started out with the idea that Berlin possessed very little of interest to us, and we strolled away to walk among the palaces and to see what was most worth seeing. Unter den Linden we were disappointed in. We stepped into the arsenal and found a full collection of armory of various ages finely arranged. In the upper part of the building a hall is being decorated as a kind of temple of fame, illustrating by its frescoes and statues the military prowess of Prussia. Although not entirely done, it is yet sufficiently finished to show its general effect. While too gorgeous with its red marble pillars, its gilt decorations, its painted walls and gilded bronze statues, to be in strictly good taste, it yet serves its general purpose, which is display. The collections of armor and uniforms upon this upper floor were more interesting to me than the guns below. Everywhere is blazoned forth the victories over the French. Captured

---

* Now Professor Armstrong of Wesleyan University at Middletown.

French flags from Sedan and Waterloo, captured guns and cannon are here displayed. The fresco, or wall-painting, representing the surrender at Sedan, is quite touching.

The National Gallery of Art, which consumed the rest of the day, interested us but little. Hardly a picture seemed to have real power. One by Louis Gallait, whose works we admired so much at Brussels—The Last Hours of Egmont—held us longer than any other.

Tuesday dawned a beautiful day, an ideal day for our trip to Potsdam. A New York lady and fellow-boarder here was glad to join us in making the trip for our company, and we were glad to have her for her superior knowledge of German. We took the ten o'clock train, which brought us to Potsdam at about eleven. We there engaged a carriage for the day and spent the rest of it in driving from point to point. We first went to Babelsberg, the present summer residence of the Emperor. The palace, built in English Gothic style, is situated in a pleasant park preserved in a natural state. The interior, which we were shown, was not beautiful, hardly attractive. A reception room, once occupied by the crown princess, was pretty, and her apartments were interesting on account of some of her own paintings. The Kaiser's bed-room and working-room were plain and adorned chiefly with family pictures.

From Babelsberg we drove to an old palace of Prince Carl, father of Frederick Charles, brother of the Kaiser. The house we were not permitted to enter, but the grounds and views from the grounds we enjoyed. Passing several places of less interest, among them the Marmor palace of Prince Wilhelm, son of the crown prince, we reached the famous park of Sans Souci. We approached on the side of the picture gallery, and this was the first building we entered. Its art treasures are not great. Many of its best pictures have been carried to the Berlin galleries, and those that remain, which are attributed to great masters, I should regard as of doubtful genuineness. The main palace was evidently built to fit its name. It is a one-storied structure in the renaissance style, and seemed to be the home of Frederick the musician, and Frederick the literateur, rather than of Frederick the general and monarch. Here are the room and the chair in which he died, here his library, a charmingly cosy, circular room, here the room occupied by his friend Voltaire. One room, decorated in porcelain flowers, was quite unique, and the fittings of all the rooms were sumptuous. The orangery was even more beautiful. The garden in front was laid out with great taste, and its fountains and rare flowers, its pond and tame fishes were a delight to the eye. One pretty conceit was a grapery in which the grape-vines were trained on trellises, ornamented by busts, giving the impression of Bacchuses. The palace itself, with its wide portico extending the length of the building, is richly adorned with statues. The central saloon is filled with copies of Raphael. Other rooms are furnished in sumptuous style.

From Sans Souci we drove to the Neues Schloss, part of which is occupied as a summer house by the crown prince. Over the beautiful waxed floors we were required to walk in felt slippers, in which we could very well skate. Here we were completely bewildered by the richness of the rooms. No wonder Frederick burned the bills incurred in erecting this immense and magnificent structure. One room which has almost driven all others from my mind, was a circular room, seventy-five or one hundred feet in diameter, the walls and pillars of which were completely encrusted in precious mineral. Quartz, agate, onyx, jasper, amethyst, malachite, garnet, amber, pearl shells and lapis lazuli were cemented together as I never supposed they existed, except in the dreams of the New Jerusalem. Twelve marble fountains adorned the sides, and immense crystal chandeliers depended from the painted ceiling. What its magnificence must be when lighted, and the fountains playing, we could only imagine.

At the Garrison Church we found the tomb of this great man who held the fate of empires in his hand.

The Stadt Schloss was very interesting, and a silver salon, whose decorations and furniture were all of silver plate, and its upholstery blue, was the prettiest room of all we saw. Divided from it by a silver balustrade, was the private cabinet of the old King, Frederick the Great, containing a curious table which could be lowered through the floor and food put on it and again hoisted, so no servant need enter the apartment. In his working-room was a desk covered with blue velvet, stained with ink, at which he wrote. A square piece cut from the desk was taken away by Napoleon, who also took the sword from his coffin.

We were late for dinner, but what cared we? The day had been delightful. All the next day I was filled with a kind of bounding joy that I was not born to royalty. It makes the pretension of the world seem hollow indeed to rap with one's cane on the coffin of Frederick the Great.

Early the next morning we went to Charlottenburg, stopping on the way at the American Exchange to read the papers. At Charlottenburg was another palace for our inspection. Like the others, it was sumptuous, indeed. The most interesting room was a salon of Queen Sophia Charlotte, decorated with blue porcelain dishes, presented to her by the merchants of London. The walls were wainscotted with dinner plates, while the fringes were of cups, saucers and vases. The satin hangings of

some of the rooms were beautiful. Yet the mausoleum
had more interest than anything else at Charlottenburg.
In it rest Frederick Wilhelm III. and his beautiful wife,
Louisa, parents of the present Emperor. The recumbant
figures, exquisitely carved from Carrara marble and
shown under blue glass, were wonderfully beautiful and
effective. Coming back we stopped for a walk in the
Thier Garden, a fine park to the west of the city, adorned
with statues, fountains, etc., but for the most part kept
as a natural forest. Here are statues of Frederick
Wilhelm III. and Queen Louisa,—the latter, recently
erected, is admirable.

From the gardens we took a carriage home, where
we arrived in time for lunch. Our afternoon sally was
to the Old Museum, where we expected to find little and
found much. The collection of original Greek and
Roman sculptures is large, surpassing that of the British
Museum. The collection of paintings, though small, is
choice. The finest Rembrandt we have seen, I think, is
Samson and his Father-in-law. The museum contains a
number of Rubens, none equal to those we have seen, yet
confirming the impression that we had formed of him.
The ringing of the four o'clock bell closed the gallery
and, going out, we took a carriage in which to complete
the day's sight-seeing. We went to the Jewish syna-
gogue, the largest in Europe, seating four thousand five

hundred persons. We then sought the bronze monument of the Great Elector, and then the remarkable statue of Frederick the Great, a marvelous work of its kind. Having stopped at the banker's we were made happy by letters, one from precious Mary. Driving out the Brandenburg gate we passed the Column of Victory, a remarkable memorial of the triumph of '70–'71, and the new Reichstag, now building. We reached the Zoological Gardens and had altogether too short a time to see its wonders. Its houses are more sumptuous than those in London, but the collection of animals I should not think as fine. One bear put out his paw in a most enticing manner, begging for something to eat. Watching the elephants eat hasty pudding was highly amusing. We were late for dinner. Evenings are usually filled with writing. I also try to improve my German a bit, and find the desire strong to settle down to a thorough study of the language. On the whole, I can use the language with more facility than I had a right to expect.

Thursday morning we awoke to a rainy day, but it did not daunt us. First I did a little shopping for necessary things, finding articles very dear. Charles and I met, by agreement, at Schloss Place and, after buying pictures, we went into the new museum. This, consisting largely of plaster casts, we did not linger over long. Six mural paintings, one, in particular, of the Huns fighting

in air, were fine. The old royal palace finished our inspection of the houses of royalty. We were hurried
through these rooms with a large party and were unable
to understand the guide. In magnificence they surpass
anything we saw at Potsdam. In fact their magnificence
cloyed. Rooms plated in gold and silver, silver thrones
and gorgeous tapestries, gold and silver plate, solid silver
columns were among the glories. The picture gallery
was very interesting, and also the Queens' room, containing the portraits of all the Prussian Queens. Here
for the first time we saw poor Queen Elizabeth, wife of
the Great Frederick. A fine picture of the present
Kaiser, and of the great elector, as well as of the beautiful Queen Louisa, claimed more attention than we could
give. The bridal chamber was interesting, and on the
marble window cases were engraved, in gold, the names
of all the royal couples here made one.

DRESDEN, 26 September.

We left Frau Fülleborn's in Berlin with real regret,
early yesterday morning. It was some compensation
that we left the German capital enveloped in rain. The
journey of three hours between Berlin and Dresden was
uninteresting. The country, for the most part, was flat.
Three Germans, one a woman, occupied the carriage with
us, and their incessant clatter was almost crazing. It all
seemed to be about fifty pfennigs.

As soon as we had removed the dust of travel we started to find the gallery, an easy matter, for it is contained in an immense building, apparently taking in a large part of the city. A glorious gallery it is, full of the richest treasures of the art of all ages and people. One thing was very noticeable, that the subjects of the paintings are almost wholly sacred or mythological; historical scenes and landscapes play a small part. Rubens is represented by some thirty pictures, nearly all of mythological subjects. In conception and execution they all fall much below those we have seen at Antwerp, Brussels or Berlin, and almost inclined me to modify the high opinion I had formed of him as an artist. The tendency to paint huge masses of flesh is, in these works, exaggerated, and in mythological scenes becomes voluptuous. His pupils, especially Jordaens, exaggerate this fault. Several of my favorite, Rembrandt, are here, two from the history of Samson and several portraits, but none so striking as the Samson at Berlin. We were very much interested in several exquisite paintings by a Dutch artist, Van Werff, the finish of which were as delicate as ivory. Among the most famous of the pictures are Correggio's La Notte and Magdalen, Guido's Christ crowned with thorns, Murillo's St. Roderiguez, Bottoni's Magdalen, Holbein's Madonna, but before and beyond every other treasure stands the

Sistine Madonna. Familiar as we have always been with reproductions of all kinds of this famous picture, it was yet a revelation. I had never dreamed of its power. Into the little room which it alone occupies, everyone comes with bated breath. All talk is in a subdued whisper, every foot-fall is hushed. The feeling of profound reverence and its manifestations are instructive. Any levity would seem like sacrilege.

The larger part of Saturday we also spent in the gallery, and an hour or more in the Grüne Gewölbe or green vault of the royal palace. The art treasures of these rooms, although of a different character from those of the gallery, are no less wonderful. In bronze, in ivory, in pearl, in amber, in gems of all kinds the collection is wonderfully rich. Cups carved from amber, whole cabinets made of the material, sabres of solid gold and mother of pearl, vases set with garnets and turquois, these were some of the many wonders. But the gems were the most dazzling. Here were arranged cases of diamonds, of rubies, of emeralds and sapphires of untold value. Swords whose hilts were a solid blaze of diamonds, a bow containing six hundred and sixty-two diamonds, the smallest being about the size of those in my ear-rings, the largest like a three cent piece! One necklace contained thirty-eight diamonds, the largest like a five cent nickel, the smallest the size of a silver three cent piece. These cases were a blaze of glory. After buying some pictures and making an attempt to buy some linen, which I found quite as dear as it would have been in America, we went home to dinner. I felt tired, and as it was raining, spent the remainder of the afternoon in reading and writing.

Sunday found me quite used up, and instead of going to church I went to bed. Monday we took an early start through the rain to the Johannessen Museum. These museums are growing painfully monotonous. This one was composed, for the most part, of arms and armour, although there were, as in the green vaults, some exquisite objects of vertu. One of the most remarkable of them was a jeweled set of back-gammon. Both the board and men were decked with pearls, emeralds, garnets and gold. It was a sight which I supposed did not exist out of fairy land, to see horses decked with harnesses set in all manner of precious stones. Here are treasured some mementos of historical interest. Here are the sword of Luther, the armor of Gustavus Adolphus, a saddle of Napoleon, a hunting horn of Henry IV., etc.

We did not see the sun in Dresden, and much of the time the rain fell as it did when we left. At the station we found the H———s, with whom we had previously traveled from Geneva to Chamounix. The insufferable courier was still with them. Poor Mama H———

begins to feel some anxiety as to how the money is going.
They had a bill for candles of one dollar and seventy-five
cents for a night at one place. Their slip-shod manner
of traveling shows very well how one may spend quan-
tities of money and get very little. They spent the
night in Dresden, stayed until noon, and did not see the
Sistine!

Prague seems old and ancient, with a bit of orient-
alism about it. We arrived before three and at once took a
carriage and drove out to find Mr. Clark, the missionary
of the American Board. This was somewhat difficult, but
we finally discovered him, and after a short visit received
his promise to call in the evening. We then drove to
the Burg, famous for having witnessed the outbreak of
the Thirty Years' War. The old Cathedral, near it, is in
process of restoration. Wallenstein's palace, still owned
by a branch of his family, had a great interest. Its
beautiful marble hall, its chapel and garden dining-room
are as the great general left them. Theckla's portrait
was on the walls, but it was growing too dark to see it.
We drove to the hotel across a fine old bridge (Karl's
Brücke), adorned with thirty or more fine statues. Some
of them are painful, as one of the crucifixion. Such
representations are extremely painful to me. I can only
hope they help some into a better life. It was hardly
home, going back to our hotel, the Englische Hof. For

the first time I felt a repugnance to sleeping in a hotel bed. The room was far from inviting, and nothing seemed attractive. The evening was spent with Mr. Clark, who talked with us most of the time about his work, which is, indeed, laborious. It gave me a better idea than I before had, of how work in Papal lands may be blessed. A large part of his work is through the dead State Protestant churches. He has been instrumental in organizing many Sunday-schools in such churches.

Tuesday morning was rainy again, but in spite of this fact we found our way out soon after breakfast. We visited the Hussite church, where Huss preached four centuries ago. Its altars and pillars were loaded with emblems of papacy. In no church have we seen so much evidence of superstition. It made me feel sick at heart. To have once known the truth and to have fallen from it, how much greater the degradation! We also did a little shopping in the garnet jewelry and glass, for which Bohemia is famed. We ordered a set of glass sent to London, but I have serious doubt whether it will ever reach its destination.

At half-past eleven we took the train for Vienna, and were packed rather closely with disagreeable people. I presume they thought we were disagreeable, for they wanted the window up and we wanted it down. The country through which the journey was made was rather interesting, different from a part of the country between Dresden and Prague, which I suppose was the outskirts of the Saxon-Switzerland. We reached Vienna about seven, rather tired. The ride from the station to our pension in Maximillian Platz was rather long, and the first pension we called at did not receive us. Twice we were stopped on the way; once for toll over a bridge, and once for customs. Vienna has customs of its own. All these countries are fearfully taxed. Even a poor boarding-house keeper must pay tax on her boarders, and no matter how small an income is, it must still be taxed.

Wednesday was largely spent in finding out what a beautiful city Vienna is. The outside of the buildings so delighted us that we were quite contented without entering them. We found the Imperial Library, a handsome museum of three hundred and fifty thousand volumes. We also visited Harrach's picture gallery, a small, private collection without much of note or merit, hardly worth climbing the stairs for. At the banker's we found our letters, a delightful treat. In the afternoon we found our way to St. Stephen's church, the most conspicuous as well as the oldest of the churches of the city. Its spire is very fine, but the inside of the church, like most Catholic houses of worship, seemed cheap and taudry in the excess of ornamentation. A walk about the Ring revealed more beauties to admire. The two new museums, the Academy of Art, the Palais de Justice, the Parliament House, the Rath House, and the University, all within a stone's throw of each other, represent probably fifty millions in money and, in beauty, are a cluster of buildings unequalled for architectural impressiveness. That the old fortifications were leveled to form the street on which these buildings are situated, is a particularly pleasing thought to an ardent peace woman. In the Volk Garten, a pretty park opposite these buildings, we found in a chaste Greek temple Canova's Theseus and the Curtain, a work of Greek simplicity and power. Near by the bronze statues of Duke Charles and Eugene of Savoy draw the attention for their vigor.

Thursday morning we gave to the Imperial Treasury. I had thought that at Dresden we had exhausted the beauty of gems and jewels, but here was a collection which charmed us for hours: the Austrian regalia, the regalia of the Holy Roman Empire, the regalia of Napoleon as King of Italy. But what could more plainly tell of the transition of life than to behold the jewels of Marie Antoinette and the cradle of the little King of Rome? Who could covet the smallest gem? Yet it was a delight and privilege to see such

dainty and delicate things. Some of the articles made of all
manner of precious minerals, such as hyacinth, jasper,
lapis lazuli, chrysolite, emerald, garnet, agate, sardonyx,
onyx, etc., were beautiful in the extreme. The royal
christening robes, heavy with pearls and gold, were
beautiful to look upon, yet on how many an unhappy
baby have they been placed. The cabinet of coins and
antiquities contained other fine gems, the cameos being
particularly fine.

In the afternoon we took a horse-car excursion to
Schönbrunn, the summer home of the Emperor. The
horse-cars here are hardly to be patronized for pleasure.
They are usually over crowded and have smoking rooms
back and front. The smoke must always be encountered,
whether one gets in or out. The tobacco traffic is
the monopoly of the government, and I suppose it is
money in its pocket to encourage the use of the weed.
The palace at Schönbrunn presented nothing wonderful
except its size. A building of numberless rooms stretches
itself over many feet of ground. Owing to the Emperor's
presence we were not able to get inside. The garden
was very pretty, tastefully decorated with statuary and
flowers. The palm house, a small crystal palace, was
very beautiful.

Friday, October 2d, we reserved for the Belvidere
picture gallery and gave to it our entire morning. The

collection is full and representative, containing more works of Italian masters than any we háve yet seen. It is particularly rich in examples of the best portrait painters. Not many Rembrandts, but it has good examples of Rubens, Van Dyke, Titian, Velasquez and Veronese. Nor are there any very famous works. Carlo Dolce's Mater, which we see so often copied, Titian's Woman taken in Adultery, are perhaps the best known. Here, too, is Titian's Ecce Homo, an unfeeling work, which tended to confirm my belief that Titian had no spiritual insight. Battoni's Prodigal Son pleased me very much. It pictured the son upon his father's breast and the father drawing his mantel about him. A Magdalen by Orazio Gentileschi, which gave me quite a different impression from that of Correggio or Battoni, was very striking; there the penitent woman has her eyes turned toward heaven. Augustus Carsaci's St. Francis was full of expression, and we admired the Presentation in the Temple by Fra Bartolommeo, the first of his works which we have seen. The gallery has a number of Guido's, which show him to have been a most unequal artist.

Saturday we finished up odds and ends. We spent our freshest hour and a half, from half-past nine until eleven, in getting into the Parliament buildings, and after we crowded in and got our tickets there was very little to see. The room of the popular branch is semi-circular, adorned with marble and furnished with ordinary desks, in no respect striking. After coming out we went to the front of the building and walked into the vestibule, a solid marble aula in the Greek style. We were allowed no further advance, and came away muttering that it does not compare with Washington's Capitol. The Art Museum, near the Parliament House, possesses a large collection of early paintings. There was very little interest to us in the collection. But the building, the Academy of Art, is very beautiful and well adapted to its purposes. In the front of it stands a fine bronze statue of Schiller. Nearly every town seems to have some monument to the poet of the people. In the afternoon we visited the Capuchins, where are the royal vaults. Near by, in the Augustinian Church, is an elaborate marble monument, by Canova, to Marie Christina, daughter of Maria Theresa. Although the separate parts seemed good, the effect of the whole was bad. We then took a carriage and had a drive of an hour to the banks of the Danube. I had expected to find the blue Danube a yellow, murky stream, but it was really blue, and the view from the Rudolph Brücke at sun-set was wholly charming.

Sunday morning we were awakened by beating of drums and blowing of bugles, and we aroused with a vague impression that it must be the Fourth of July. It proved to be the Emperor's patron saint's day, and in the Votive Church, opposite our house, early services were held which the military attended with grand parade. We found for ourselves a little Scotch Presbyterian chapel, where we heard an excellent sermon from Professor Solman, of Aberdeen. His theme was the first Psalm, and he cut down deep into character and life: good, honest preaching. The afternoon was spent in writing, but in the evening we had a treat.

I don't know that I always regard missionary concerts as a treat, but of a Sunday evening, in a far away city, they partake of this character. Into the house came, on Friday, Dr. Post and Mrs. Post and their little boy, on their way back to Beyrut. A Miss Kelly, whom we had previously met at Edinburgh, and who is thoroughly interested in all good words and works, is in the house for the winter. Dr. Dennis and Mrs. Dennis, also of Beyrut, are lodged near by. When we planned our meeting we thought of having the Posts and Miss Kelly, but Dr. Post invited the Dennises, and brought in a young Dr. Glover, who returns with him as instructor. Dr. Glover brought a young English doctor, who is on his way as medical missionary to Bagdad, and Dr. Dennis brought too Dr. Henschel, who is the chaplain of the English Embassy, and who has been offered the Bishopric of Jerusalem. Frau Lejeune and

Fraulein Schneider came in to swell the number to eleven. To meet such cultured, scholarly men, who have done such a vast work, broadens one's ideas of foreign missions. Dr. Post's work has been stupendous. He has collected fifty thousand specimens of Syrian flowers, and arranged and published in Arabic a complete Flora. He has also published several other Arabic textbooks. The observatory at Beyrut is connected with those at Vienna, Berlin and London for meteorological observations. The hospital of the German order of St. John is under the general supervision of the medical faculty of the college. We were particularly interested in the account of the abandonment of the vernacular as the basis of instruction in the college. Dr. Henschel is interested in prophecy, and stayed until eleven fitting Scripture to oriental inscriptions and making out the approaching end of all things.

To take the train from Vienna for Munich at seven forty-five required early rising. But we screwed our courage to the sticking-place and did it. It was with real regret that we left this beautiful capital. Our home with Frau Lejeune was very pleasant. She and her sisters were true ladies, and showed us great courtesies. In leaving Vienna we left Austria. The country apparently differs little from Germany. It, like its neighbor, is burdened with an immense army. The people differ in appearance quite a good deal from the Prussians. They incline to be dark, sallow and *wiry*. Vienna is a more cosmopolitan city than Berlin ; English and French are more generally spoken, and more nationalities are seen in the streets. Oriental costumes are by no means uncommon. It is, too, a gayer place. Evidently the theatre and opera play a more important part in the life of the people.

From Vienna to Munich was a twelve hours' ride, and we were obliged to make three changes. The carriages were not good, the roads were rough, and a part of the way the train was slow. It seemed strange that the day train between two so important capitals should not be better equipped. It was like going from Franklin to Aroostock county. We were, a part of the way, interested in the antics of a newly wedded couple. The naiveté of the bride was quite charming, especially when she leaned over and implanted a kiss on her bridegroom's lips, or gave me a full account of herself. There was also a good natured German, who regarded us with curious interest and expressed undisguised amazement that we were not to dine all day. Yet, on the whole, the day was tedious. The scenery was pretty, but not striking ; the land rich and well tilled. At Munich we found rooms at Frau Bürger's, who seemed the personification of good humor and easy going nature.

Her pension was hardly a model of neatness and elegance, but we concluded we could endure it for a week, yet I should be sorry to be condemned for a winter to her tender mercies. The bed felt good, even the intolerable feather beds were welcome, and we soon sought them. Our conscientious methods in sight seeing did not allow any extra nap in the morning, and by nine we were off for the banker's. Here good news from home awaited us.

The days at Munich we filled as full as possible, for the city offered greater attractions than we had supposed. It is really the finest German city we have seen. The streets are broad and the buildings, though not beautiful, are neat and substantial. The squares are numerous, and adorned with fitting monuments and statues. The König's Platz is beautiful by reason of its buildings in purest Greek style. The Sieges Thor is so massive that one could through it appreciate something of the power of Greek architecture. We found our way into the courts of the royal residence, and joined ourselves to a party who were going we knew not whither, but it proved to be a tour of the palace, which we had not intended making. We were repaid by the frescoes by Schnorr, which in one room depicted scenes from the life of Charlemagne, and in another from the life of Barbarossa. The dance hall was very beautiful, walled in solid marble of exquisite tints. Most of the rooms were like those in all palaces, dreary enough in their faded magnificence. The new Pinakothek next drew us. Here we found a beautiful collection of porcelain painting. Wonderfully beautiful and expressive seemed the faces thus portrayed. The paintings in oil were for the most part the work of the Munich school, and contained some pieces of great power. The Destruction of Jerusalem, by Kaulbach; the Death of Wallenstein, by Piloty, were among the greatest. As I compare paintings of the modern school with these of the ancient it seems to me the former fail in the selection of topics. Some great truth must lie behind a great picture. After dinner we sallied forth to find Herr Tauber and his family. I am not sure that I left any clear impression upon their minds beside the fact that I spoke abominable German, but I think they were pleased to meet some one who had so recently seen their mother and sister. Herr Tauber seemed anxious to do something for us, so he accompanied us to the bronze factory. Here we at once felt at home, for the first objects we saw were the legs of Daniel Webster, and on looking about we recognized many friends, including Washington, Patrick Henry, Jefferson, Lincoln, Everett, Peabody, and others. Indeed, the larger part of the models were to fill orders from America. The bronze doors of the Capitol, the Cincinnati fountain, the Emancipation Group, at Washington, as well as many other of our best bronze statues were made here.

Wednesday morning before nine o'clock Herr Tauber called, who had kindly offered to visit with us the Glyptothek and the Old Museum. The Glyptothek delighted us exceedingly. Its collection of Greek and Roman statuary is not only large, but in a remarkable state of preservation. I will confess to having been more pleased with the statues from the pediment of the Temple at Ægina than with the Elgin marbles. The figures were very perfect, although in parts they have been restored, but restored by Thorwaldsen. The building is extremely beautiful and the taste of the arrangement beyond criticism. The halls were *pillared* in marble and vaulted in gold and pale tints of green or blue. The Old Museum, was to me hardly as interesting as the Dresden Gallery, although standing close up to it. It has no one great picture to place beside the Sistine Madonna. In it, however, we saw Dürer at his best, in his Four Evangelists, Paul being the finest. A picture attributed to Massys, if it really were his work, would go far to reconciling us to his reputation. It was an altar piece of the Entombment, and both in delicacy of conception and execution is worthy of great praise. Guido Reni's Assumption seemed to us among the best of the pictures. Its coloring and expression, as well as its conception, are admirable. Here Murillo can be studied with advantage. All but one of his pieces are *genre*, and that is a picture of a monk. Here also is a large collection of the exquisitely finished pictures of Van Werff. But we had not time enough for this gallery. We needed to revisit it and to linger.

In the afternoon we turned our faces to the museum of fossils connected with the University, said to be the fullest in existence, and indeed beside them all fossils which I have ever seen sink into nothingness. My ignorance, which every day grows more colossal, prevented anything like a proper appreciation of the value of these tales of the rocks. The hipparion, ancestor of the horse, was among the most interesting of these long-extinct animals.

The days in Munich were full and exhausting. We were glad of extra rest on Thursday morning. In departing we left some pleasant people behind us. At ten o'clock we started for the station and at a quarter before eleven were on the way to Verona, a thirteen-hour trip. The roads were rough and the carriages not over-comfortable, yet the day wore on. We skirted the Tyrol, which we entered at Innspruck, and made the Brunner pass, four thousand feet high, before dark. The scenery of the Tyrol we enjoyed as much as the Alps. The air and clouds were in a condition to give the best effects. The autumn tints gave a new touch to the landscape, and the snow-capped mountains laid a background for the whole. The flood of a week ago had carried away a bridge just beyond Bozen and here, in the dark, we were obliged to get out and, by the aid of flaming torches, to cross a plank bridge over the ravine. It was a picturesque sight and the first experience of anything out of the natural course which we have had.

But all things come to an end, and even journeys to Verona, which include two custom house examinations. The ride through the streets of this ancient city at nearly midnight was a strange experience. We passed through heavy walls and under low Roman arches, and between the high stone walls of the houses which bounded the narrow streets. It was easy to transport ourselves back to the days of Bocaccio, and we almost expected to see a Romeo under some window singing his farewell to his Juliet. I am glad we had this touch of Verona by night. In the morning, as we rode about, the illusion had vanished with the flood of sunlight. Here, indeed, was the monster arena built in the reign of Diocletian, but under its portals shop-keepers were busy. Here were the Roman arches which had stood for nearly two thousand years, but under them Yankee horse-cars were plying and to them telegraph wires were attached. Here were the palaces of nobles and philosophers, but to them were affixed advertisments of Singer Sewing Machines. So the daylight revealed that we were not in the middle ages. We went to Juliet's tomb, and here we found that irreverent visitors had cast their visiting cards. The home of the Capulets did not look just as it is represented on the stage, nor just as our favorite garden scene in Society hall, which was got up with special reference to the lover of this immortal twain. Even the balcony was not there.

It was a wretchedly slow train which took us from Verona to Venice. Seventy-one miles dragged out through four hours, so that really the best of the day was consumed in the trip, for it was nearly three when our eyes rested on this wondrous city of the sea. I expected Venice would be different from anything I had ever seen, and was prepared to be charmed. But I hardly expected anything so different and so charming. The long bridge of two miles brought us to the Island city and to one end of the great canal. At the station were drawn up long rows of gondolas which, with their black hulks and coverings like funeral palls, looked more like a hearse than anything else. In the stern stood the gondolier and, sitting with our back to him, we glided noiselessly along, as though impelled by an unknown power. In and out of small canals and large canals we sped, hardly noticing anything and only feeling into what a strange life we had entered. Our gondolier might have been Charon, our canal the Styx, and our haven Acheron, for all likeness they bore to any previous experiences. Here is a city without streets, without dust or mud, without garden or parks, without horses or dogs, without the sound of a passing foot or driving team, a city alive and yet from which all ordinary signs of life are banished.

The Pension Suisse gave us a pleasant room on the Grand canal and an excellent lunch, to which we were prepared to do justice. Immediately, as our appetites were satisfied, we stepped into our gondola and started to explore the Grand canal and the colonies of Venice. The houses and palaces present a strange melange of ancient splendor and present decay. Where once the nobles dwelt now tradesmen ply their business. But neither time nor neglect can wholly dim the wonderful architectural remains of this queer city. We entered a church and there saw how totally different is the Christian ideal in building houses of worship from that of the North. The dome has supplanted the tower and the spire, and the most sumptuous and ornate embellishment the severe plainness of Gothic art.

Sunday, 11 October.

Here is a little time in which to look back over the ground we have covered. Germany is behind us. On the whole the impression left is not one of pleasure. Grand and big and eminent as is this country, its characteristics are not pleasing. Its type of civilization is powerful and material and is represented in its extremes by its army, four hundred and fifty thousand strong, by its enormous consumption of beer, by its feather-beds, and by its universities with their materialistic and ideal philosophies.

To begin with, we saw no sign of religious life, by which I mean spiritual, vital piety. Berlin had the finest churches of any city of any size I was in. Sunday is a work-day for the many, a feast-day for the few. The state religion seems purely formal and includes mechanical baptism, mechanical confirmation and automatic instruction in the schools, while unbelief and skepticism of all kinds are running riot. The men seem made of coarse clay and are boorish in manners. The life of a woman is too hard to be viewed with anything but indignation. In addition to the duties of the house, the women have laid upon them all kinds of the hardest, most menial and degrading labor. In many parts of the country a basket strapped upon the back seemed an integral part of her dress, and in it she carried all kinds of burdens, from vegetables to heavy boxes and huge piles of wood. To see a woman in the rain, barefooted, bareheaded and bearing a heavy burden, was a common sight. Yet they seem a healthy race. That they are is a fact which controverts all my preconceived ideas of hygiene. They hate fresh air in their houses, they drink beer and live on sausage, sleep under and on feather-beds, their children are half-clothed, with bare legs, arms and necks, and yet they are pictures of health. They are a hardy race.

I dread for German ideas to take a firmer hold of American life. I feel sure that they are subversive of the best type of character and civilization. Not much in common have these burly denizens of the North with the dark-eyed, graceful, light-hearted Italians. No wonder the Latin race perished before the northern invader, no wonder art died and learning languished. We are but yet in the confines of Italy, but already we can see what different ideas and ideals have ruled here. So far we are simply bewildered. Our yesterday was spent in St. Mark's, in the Ducal Palace, in the Rialto, in a gondola and in the shops. Impressions are too novel to be analyzed; we must traverse the ground again. One spot we shall not revisit. It is the prison of the Ducal Palace and the Bridge of Sighs. Down, down we went through a narrow corridor of solid masonry. On either side were cells of utter darkness, lined with wood and furnished with a plank bed. A hole in the wall admitted food, and opposite this, in the corridor, a niche was seen, on which were placed a crucifix and candle : sole spot of light. Down, still down we went to the lowest depths, reserved for political offenders. Here no wood lined the cells, no plank served as bed, no crucifix lighted the utter darkness. Who entered here, abandoned hope. He passed the massive stone bridge, walled, covered and grated, and turned his back on mercy. In the walls are seen the holes which fastened the rivets of the guillotine, and just beyond, crowning horror, three holes open to the sea, gave to this silent keeper of horrors the blood of the victim. As we paused, a suppressed gurgle reached our ears, as though, in vain, the guardian of foul secrets were struggling to speak and to tell the story.

Our Sunday was spent very quietly, but in no way can we make a Sunday abroad a real Sabbath. We went to the English chapel, climbing four flights of stairs. The sermon was an indifferent prayer-meeting talk, yet it presented Christ as the only hope of salvation. The afternoon we spent in writing. In the evening the gondoliers, their boats decorated with gay lanterns, rowed up and down the canal, singing. I fear the music was not of a sacred character, but it had picturesque features.

Tuesday Evening.

This is our last night in Venice, and it is time to gather up impressions and to put them in form. Venice is more than I had dreamed or fancied. The air of perpetual youth, the apparent absence of toil or care, the holiday appearance of men and things, foster the illusion which the first sight of the city gives, that one has passed the limits of our every-day world and entered the realms of another planet. After the general impression had been taken and we began to study in detail, the peculiar and grand architecture of the city claimed attention. Here we met a type of architecture, as exhibited in the churches, quite different from anything we had before seen. The Gothic is replaced by the Byzantine, and the severe chaste interior adornment by a wild exuberance of sumptuous detail. This characteristic is seen carried to its height in St. Mark's. Its seven domes surmount an elaborately decorated pile in which marbles of all hues and the richest mosaics and intricate carvings are united. The interior is a mass of exquisite workmanship. Hardly a square inch can be found on which the artist has not wrought. In marble, in mosaic, in wood and stone carving and in bronze, its decorations may be found. The light is admitted by windows in the domes, so small as to be hardly perceptible. The effect is dark, but not gloomy, simply rich. The most effective work to me is the head of Christ, in mosaic, over the portal. To study St. Mark's in any fitting way is the work of weeks. I did not study it enough to feel that it is a Christian church.

Venice presents a domestic architecture no less striking and unique. A ride through the Grand Canal tells better than any words the character of these old, noble Venetians. Other cities adorn their palaces and churches, these men adorned their dwellings worthily, in the highest and richest art. One can not but regret, in visiting Venice in 1885, that his was not the privilege to have seen it in 1585. One is constantly filled with amazement in view of what this people was and did. I cannot help believing that their conscientious piety was a large element in their success in all lines of endeavor. The pious care of the Venetian for the relics of St. Mark, which forms so prominent a place in the city's history, is not without significance. The adoring attitude in which the Doges are painted has a meaning,— Venice was the queen of the sea, but the subject of the Holy One.

The paintings of the Ducal Palace introduces us to Venetian art at its best. After seeing the Titians, Tintorettos and Veroneses there I felt I had not seen these artists before. In Titian's figure of Truth, the center of a large canvas, I felt for the first time that Titian may have had some spiritual insight, but even here it was wanting. The execution and coloring of the picture are beyond compare. I am almost inclined to rank second in the paintings of the Ducal Palace Giorgione's

Christ Enthroned. Tintoretto's Paradise required more
study than we could give. Yet we felt its power. There
is an upward, strong movement in the picture, which,
notwithstanding its immense number of figures, is not
fantastic. This canvas, eighty-five feet long, is believed
to be the largest single canvas in existence.

This morning we visited San Giorgio Maggiore. The
wood carvings (Flemish) of the choir stalls are the richest we have seen. There is also in this church a magnificent group in bronze, representing the Holy Family,
upon a globe supported by the four evangelists. The
figure of the father, irreverent as seems the attempt,
is one of singular grace and majesty. Connected with
this church was formerly a Benedictine monastery, destroyed by Napoleon. It is strange how we have traced
the blighting and destroying influence of that man
throughout Europe. Yet I sometimes think he did some
good, by the over-ruling power of Providence, in breaking the hold of the idea of the divine right of kings
and of the infallibility of the church upon the popular
mind. The fact that he made the Pope a prisoner and
played foot ball with the crowned heads of Europe, even
grinding the remains of the Holy Roman Empire to
dust, must have made an impression not to be outgrown.
And he was a Corsican boy of humble birth.

Of course we visited the lace and glass factories.

My head was so turned by their bewildering charms that I lost much sleep. The lace factory under government control manufactures no less than thirty-four kinds of old Venetian lace. It was quite an education to study them. Glass we found exorbitant. We have not bought a piece. The process of making was very interesting.

Wednesday Morning.

In rather a melancholy mood we started out for our farewell view of the Queen city of the sea. We turned our faces toward the Campanile in St. Mark's Place, in order that we might obtain a comprehensive view. On the way I stopped to feed the doves which swarmed upon me in great numbers, lighting upon my hands, arms, shoulders, anywhere that they could get a pick at the corn in my hands. The ascent of the Campanile was not by stairs, but by an ascending plane, and was very easy. We feasted our eyes upon the panorama until I am sure Venice will always have a place in our memories. At the Piazzetta we took a gondola and visited the Church of dei Frari, which has monuments to Titian and Canova. The first is a fine work containing, in bas relief, his Assumption. The other, very similar to the monument executed by Canova for the daughter of Maria Theresa at Vienna, merits all of Ruskin's criticisms. Near the church is the Scuola Rocco, a handsome hall containing many of Tintoretto's pictures. Unfortunately we had not time to make much of a study of them. "The Crucifixion" and "Annunciation" are best known. We were not able to see Tintoretto through Mr. Ruskin's eyes, although the ass feeding on withered palm leaves in the former picture is striking.

A hasty lunch,—and we were soon at the station, whence the one o'clock train bore us to Bologna, where we arrived in the midst of a pouring rain at a little past five.

Thursday morning we made our first visit to the gallery, walking, and seeing the leaning towers and much of interest. Nearly all the shops are built with arcades, which form a complete defence from rain. The city surprised us by its cleanliness. It seemed as clean a city as we had been in. The gallery was a surprise to us in the general excellence of its pictures. No gallery we have yet seen has a better average. First in order of merit doubtless is the St. Cecilia of Raphael. Strangely enough this picture, unlike the Sistine Madonna, seemed to us better in the engravings of it than in the original. This is owing to the violent colors in which the figures are represented, all against a heavy, blue sky. The other pictures were mainly of artists of the Bolognese school. Chief stands Guido, admirably represented in his Crucifixion, and Piatà (which contains his celebrated Matre Dolerosa), as well as in many other works of merit.

A Samson was particularly good. We had here our first glimpse of Domenichino in two admirably painted works, but with unfortunately repellant subjects. Lodovico Carracci's Transfiguration was a work of great power, as well as a picture by Guercino, representing two Carthenians in the desert worshiping the Virgin. Several other Virgins enthroned were excellent. One by Annibale Carracci especially attracted me. We were very much interested in pictures of great merit painted by a young woman, a pupil of Guido, Elizabetta Sirani, who died at the age of twenty-six. Her conception of the Magdalen is one of the best we have seen. She is clothed in a sack-cloth garment and gazes tearfully on a crucifix.

From the gallery we went to the civic museum, in which is stored and admirably arranged a large collection of Etruscan relics which have been recently unearthed. I confess to something of my daughter's contempt for a "museum of dirty dishes," but regard it as a manifestation of my ignorance. Very interesting, however, was the ancient university building adjoining, now used as a city library. It is a forcible reminder of the time when Bologna gathered ten thousand students and the greatest philosophers of the age. The court was unique and interesting in its being completely covered with the arms of its distinguished professors and students. The hall formerly used for an anatomical demonstration room was interesting in its quaint ceiling of cedar wood, carved to represent the signs of the Zodiac or, rather, constellations. In this room Galvani performed his experiments. In the Church of San Petronio Charles V. was crowned.

Back to the hotel, dinner, an omnibus ride to the station ; and after waiting an hour for a delayed train we were on our way to Florence. It was so late when we arrived that we went to a hotel instead of our pension and passed a night made uncomfortable by hideous street noises.

Early Friday morning we sought our Pension Chapman in the Via Pandolfini, near where Dante was born and Tito found by Bratti. Our hostess proved to be a Salem woman, full of pluck and energy, as lively as a cricket at the age of sixty-eight. Her American breakfasts are a great improvement over the continental roll and coffee.

The first visit was to the banker's and we learned the horrible news of Beth's fatal accident. It is the first shadow which has crossed our path. Everything seemed changed, and it was some time before I could control myself to go out. We made a day at the Uffizi, of which criticisms are reserved until the second visit. Coming back we visited the Loggia dei Lanzi, which has some interesting monuments, including one of Judith, in bronze, by Danatello. We also stepped into the court of the Vecchio palace. Its columns were most exquisitely carved. We had only time to prepare for dinner and the evening was spent in reading. Romola is our light reading and it is a charming companion.

We find here a party of eight young ladies from an Ohio seminary, under the care of a teacher. We enjoy them very much. Saturday morning, by an early start, we got to the Duomo at nine. Of this wonderful Cathedral and accompanying Campanile it is difficult to know what to say. It is safe to affirm that its likeness was never seen elsewhere. Its hugeness is the first thing which strikes the beholder. The immense octagonal dome and the far stretching nave unite in producing an astounding whole. The variegated color of its exterior produce a bizarre effect not altogether pleasing. Nor does the interior give anything of surpassing interest. To me the adjacent Baptistry is more interesting. It, too, has a mosaic exterior. Its interior is impressive. The chief objects to draw the attention are Ghiberti's far-famed doors, which, strict truth requires it to be said, need sapolio. Of the Campanile hardly too much can be said in praise. It is not a church, and no objection exists to making it a museum of the cunning skill of artists. At ten o'clock we went to the Pitti Gallery, and returned through the Uffizi, of which more later.

Letters at noon brought the news that our darling

Beth, after much suffering, passed away Friday, October 2. It is so sudden. As the most in accord with our feelings we took a long drive along the Viale dei Colli. It seemed like a bit of the paradise to which she has gone. The broad road was lined with roses and hedges, and overlooked the city, the distant mountains and the valley of the Arno. We passed the fortifications built by Michael Angelo, and the tower in which Galileo made his observations, and the house where he died.

Sunday, 18 October.

In the morning we attended the Free Church of Scotland, and heard a vigorous sermon from Dr. McDougall, in true Scotch style, on what Charles called the geometry of salvation: the nature of saving faith, the object, the exercise, the results.

Much of the afternoon and evening we spent in writing, but took a long walk to the Old Cemetery,—a beautiful spot to leave cherished dust, if left it must be, under a foreign sky. Here we found the tombs of Mrs. Browning and of Arthur Clough.

Our Monday morning was very rich. Having decided to try to get to Rome by Wednesday night, we were obliged to utilize the moments. By half past eight we were on our way to Santa Croce, and having saturated our minds with Ruskin's descriptions were prepared to explore every nook and cranny of this old Franciscan church. The façade is new and of marble, but it is the interior which attracts the student. At first sight one sees only a bare, white-washed, barn-roofed edifice, with numerous tombs skirting the sides. But when one is told that under that white-wash are waiting to be revealed some of the most exquisite paintings of Giotto and his followers, he can see what the church once was and what it will be. In several of the minor chapels chemicals have been applied and the ancient pictures in all their beauty shine forth. The most interesting of these to me, Ruskin notwithstanding, was that adorned with scenes from the lives of the two Johns. Yet it must be confessed some of the scenes from the life of St. Francis are, notwithstanding their restoration, of great power and beauty. The tombs which Ruskin reviles cover immortal dust and point to this church as the future Westminster of Italy. Here are buried Michael Angelo, Galileo, Alfieri, Macchiavelli, and others of less fame. Dante, too, has here a fine memorial. The tomb over which Ruskin raves was amusing. Yet I do believe his principles are right in spite of the sometimes absurd application of them.

Next came St. Mark's. The church itself appeared slightly interesting, but the adjoining convent, now suppressed and used as a museum, was full of suggestions. It was here Savonarola lived and

Romola saw her brother die. The frescoes of the cloisters were interesting, several by Fra Angelico full of delicacy of conception and execution. The upper floor, having the cells of the monks, gave us an idea, and the best we have had, of how these old monks lived. The cells were not as forbidding as I had supposed, and being on the second floor were free from that darkness and dampness with which the cells of monks are associated. Each cell had its frescoes, and these were interesting less as works of art than as suggestions of the type of Christianity which was prevalent in that age. Nearly all were representations of some phase of the passion of our Lord, or were taken from the legendary lives of the saints or of the Virgin. It is a remarkable fact that the works of Christ, any miracle or teaching, are rarely represented in church or convent. He is always represented as a passive sufferer, never as an active man. Query: has our religion run to the opposite extreme? Savonarola's cells were full of melancholy interest. Here was a fragment from the pyre on which he was burned, here his crucifix and hair shirt. Here also was an excellent portrait by Fra Bartolommeo. A hasty run into the Accademia, to see Michael Angelo's David, finished our morning's work.

After a night of rain, our last morning in Florence opened fair. Again we took an early start, and this time for Santa Maria Novella the Dominican church, as Santa Croce is Franciscan. The frescoes of most interest were those of Ghirlandajo (scenes from the life of Mary and of John Baptist) in the choir. A Madonna of Cimabue in one of the elevated side chapels is famous as the best work of that early artist. What we enjoyed most were the cloisters. Here were two sets, one very large, both elaborately frescoed. Now the place is used as a military school. The Government has suppressed all monasteries and confiscated much of their property. Off the first cloisters was the chapel Spagnuoli covered with curious frescoes, and having a fine echo. The Medici chapel of Lorenzo was our next point of attack. The tombs of Lorenzo and Guiliano de' Medici, by Michael Angelo, all unfinished, were of great interest. The figure of Lorenzo, sometimes called Il Pensiero, was to me very full of power. The Chapel of the Princes, built as a tomb house for the Medici, on which twenty-two million lire have been expended though it is still unfinished, was a marvel to behold. At first, as a whole, it is not pleasing, owing to the combination of colors in the marbles with which it is walled ; but an examination of the marbles and precious stones reveals their great beauty. No less than eighteen different varieties are used, and some specimens, as of the serpentine and petrified woods, are very beautiful. The library, the great Laurenzian library, once the property of the Medici, containing ten thousand manuscript volumes, was extremely interesting as showing the type of libraries in the days before books were the possession of the people. All these volumes were chained to the desks on which they were placed.

The afternoon I stayed in and wrote and rested, and the morning of Wednesday we left at eight thirty-five for Rome.

The ride was pleasant. So far I find it hard to get into the spirit of these historic spots. I have to pinch myself to realize that I am on the plains which Hannibal crossed, and not on an Iowa prairie. To approach Rome in the steam cars, and to be met by the commonplace porters and drivers, all this made the place seem a vulgar, modern city. And like a modern city does it seem on first appearance. The Via Nazionale, on which our pension is situated, might be in Detroit for all signs seen of ancient life. But on almost every corner one stumbles on some signs of ancient or mediæval Rome, and it is with these remains and with the treasures of art that we are chiefly concerned.

Rome, 25 October.

We have now been three days in Rome. We have not felt in the best of trim physically. Our first point was St. Peter's. We spent Thursday morning there and saw it only long enough to be overwhelmed, and not long enough for distinct impressions. We climbed to the roof, which is a village in itself. One afternoon was spent in a drive which included the Pincian Hill, the Corso, the Trajan Forum and the Roman, the Coliseum, the Ghetto, the Theatre of Marcellus, and the Cenci Palace. Friday morning we visited the Sistine Chapel and saw the pictures and frescoes of the Vatican, of which more hereafter.

Saturday morning we started out at nine and visited two churches, that of S. Pietro in Vincoli and Maria Maggiore. The first is notable for its statue of Moses, by Michael Angelo, part of a tomb intended for Julius II. It seems to me I never have seen marble so instinct with life. I looked at that figure, full of the righteous wrath of a just man against sin, until it seemed to me he must spring to his feet. The other church, containing no great monument, is yet in itself a monument. Incorporated into a more modern edifice are the remains of one of the oldest Christian churches, dating from the fifth century. The church itself is not to be despised as modern, for it antedates most other churches. It is modeled after the basilica, although small arches divide its beautiful white marble columns. The interior is impressive from its grandeur, and the Sistine Chapel in the right transept from the sumptuousness of its adornment. We descended to the crypt which contains the remains of the ancient church, among which was a marble group representing the Adoration, which dates from the fourth century.   The mosaics which form a fringe about the columns of the church are of exquisite workmanship, and it was with great regret we left the church half seen.

The Capitoline Museum was our next point.   Here I had it impressed upon me how incapable plaster is of reproducing marble.   Many times as I have seen casts of the dying gladiator, I have never seen anything of the power of this work.   One could look at it for hours, and all the time the heart is bleeding in sympathy for the noble, proud spirit here biting the dust.   The Faun of Praxiteles, the Venus of the Capitol, the Antinous, appealed to me as the best, as they are the most famous, of the sculptures here deposited.   The Palace of the Conservatori, opposite the Museum, contains a greater variety of Roman remains.   Its tablets, its bronzes, its statues, its inscriptions, all made ancient Rome seem real indeed.   The magnificent reliefs, formerly in an arch dedicated to Marcus Aurelius, the bronze wolf of the Capitol, the bronze boy extracting a thorn, interested me most.   Among the pictures in the gallery were many so pleasing that they would have justified a much longer stay than we gave. The frescoes of Spagna, representing Apollo and the

Muses, were pleasing. A Madonna of Francia was very attractive. Two excellent Van Dykes, miserably placed, look out amid the darkness. An unfinished Guido and his St. Sebastian appeal to one. An enormous picture by Guercino, St. Petronella, is striking, although it did not stir me as some scenes do.

The afternoon of Saturday was full of absorbing and melancholy interest. In it we rode out through the gate which looks toward Ostia, to the reputed scene of Paul's final triumph. We rode by the gate, leaving the Protestant cemetery on our right guarded by the sombre pyramid which marks the tomb of Caius Cestius, and which cast its shadow upon the great Apostle as he entered upon his last journey. A more melancholy, dismal, drear place than this deserted Roman campagna is seldom seen. It can hardly be merely its associations and the memories of what it once was that cast so dreary a shade over its face. Scarcely a human habitation breaks the mile and a half which lies between the gate and the presumed site of Paul's grave. Half way out is a little chapel, said to mark the place where Paul and Peter parted when on their way to execution. The Church of St. Paul is very disappointing as one approaches. It might well pass for a railroad station. But once inside one is overcome by its simple grandeur. It is in the form of the basilica, and for the first time I felt how this form of architecture may be inspiring and uplifting in its strength and purity. The roof of the nave and aisles is supported by four rows of twenty-one pillars of the finest Corinthian order. Their polished granite surfaces reflect the glory of the place and the marble of the wainscotting as well. Above the pillars run as a frieze the portraits of the Popes, in rich mosaic, and, still above, frescoes represent scenes in the life of the Apostle. The pillars supporting the altar roof are of exquisite oriental alabaster, as beautiful as a gem. The roof, heavily gilded, seems a little oppressive, and detracts from the upward lift of the sanctuary. The cloisters, with their delicate tints and carved columns, form an exquisite bit of architecture, but are evidently in a state of neglect.

A mile and a half beyond, at the traditional place of the execution of Paul, are three churches. The first, St. Mary of the Ladder, (Scala Caeli), has very little interest beyond a few ancient and exquisite mosaics. The second, which marks the suppositious site of the execution, is elaborately adorned with marble and with a fine mosiac floor. The marble block upon which Paul suffered was shown to us by a very pleasant monk, one of the forty Benedictines who reside in the adjoining monastery! The spot is called Tre Fontane, from the legend that three fountains sprang from the earth at three spots touched by the head of St. Paul. There is something pitiable in the way the Roman Church has overlaid the truth of Christian history with puerile fables. It seems as though the simple truths of our blessed gospel were grand enough without smothering them in the wrapping of such senseless traditions. I sometimes long for a second set of the epistles of Paul.

Our Sunday was quietly spent. In the morning we went to the Scotch church, where about ten worshipers gathered. It takes very poor preaching to spoil the gospel, but that poor preacher almost did it.

Monday we made a full day, starting as soon as possible after breakfast for the Borghese Gallery, a gallery said to be the best private collection of pictures in the world. All the pictures in Italy suffer for the want of being well hung, but we provided ourselves with opera glasses to-day, and were determined not to lose more than was necessary. The most famous paintings in this gallery are, perhaps, the Danae, of Correggio, and the Sacred and Profane Love, of Titian. The pictures I find lingering in my memory are St. Stanislaus and the infant Christ by Ribera, a Madonna by Francia, and a Crucifixion by Van Dyke.

We had time enough to drive to the Corsini palace. Although the collection is inferior in number and reputation to the Borghese Gallery, we yet found many works to interest. Among the pictures Murillo's Madonna

is " facile princeps." Carlo Dolce's Madonna seemed
to us one of his best works. Guercino's St. Jerome,
his Ecce Homo, and Guido Reni's Herodias, are
among the best of the collection. The afternoon
we gave to churches. First we took Gesu, the
Church of the Jesuits. It is the most elaborately adorned
church we have yet seen. It did not attract me.
Still, to stand by the ashes of Loyola was something.
The altar over his grave is sumptuous in the extreme.
The pillars supporting the cover to the altar are of lapis
lazuli, and a ball of the same stone surmounting the
whole could be hardly less than three feet in diameter.

The Church of Maria in Aracoeli on the Capitol Hill,
was our next point. Each church seems to surpass all
others in gorgeousness in some respect. Here it was the roof,
so rich, so grand, so gorgeous in its gilt that the rest of
the modest little church was quite put to shame. It is
at this church that the wonderful Bambino is kept, and
from here he proceeds in solemn state to the houses of the
sick where his miraculous cures are made. We peti-
tioned to see him, and were solemnly conducted into one
of the chapels of the sacristy. The priest, who I suppose was Bambino's own servant, drew back the
doors of a manger and showed a white and gilt casket,
which, being unlocked and opened, revealed upon its
white satin tufting a bundle covered with rich swaddling

clothes. The priest then invited us to kneel and make a prayer to the image, but we were excused upon explaining that we were Protestants. Whereupon he fell upon his knees and uttered a prayer, ending by kissing the feet of the baby. When the Bambino was unswathed a wooden doll by no means ugly was exposed, appareled in the richest garments covered with all kinds of jewels which had been presented by those whom he had blessed. Strange, strange sight! It may differ from idolatry, but we could not see the difference. The signs of Mariolatry are here very noticeable. I read a prayer in this church largely made up of ascriptions to the Virgin, to whom the prayer was addressed. She was called mother and daughter of God, bride of the Holy Spirit, etc.

We next drove to St. Clement, interesting for its age. Here a Christian church of the ninth century rests upon an earlier one of the fourth century, which in turn was built upon the ruins of a pagan temple. To the first we descended. To the second, which has been excavated, one can not go on account of the water. The early frescoes which we there found were interesting and not without some artistic merit. Some of the pillars were very beautiful, a few of them being taken from the pagan temple.

Tuesday, 27 October.

A glorious morning soon clouded into rain. We started early for the Catacomb of St. Agnes, about a mile beyond the wall by the Porta Pia, through which Victor Emanuel entered the city. This gate, built by and bearing the name of Pius VI., now bears an inscription to the memory of those soldiers who fell for the unity of their fatherland. Poor Pope! I don't wonder he shuts himself up in the Vatican, sole remnant of his once universal power. We descended forty-five steps to the Church of St. Agnes, an ancient basilica, having little of interest save some mosaics of the ninth century in the tribune. We had provided ourselves with candles, and followed our guide down into an apparently dark cellar by a double flight of steps. Unfortunately he spoke neither French nor English, but most of his Italian we could understand. This catacomb is well excavated and well preserved. Through a labyrinth of narrow passes we wandered, on each side of us being the tiers of walled-up graves, or, rather, of tombs. Many of these were undisturbed, and were sealed, some with marble, some with terra cotta, some with stone. The inscriptions on many could be plainly read. For the most part they were simple, only giving name and date with some expression of Christian faith. The words "in pace," "victoria in pace" were common, but most frequent was the cross or some symbol, as an olive leaf or a dove. In some of the graves which had been opened were gathered vases and lamps and other articles, some of which, I judged, had been interred with the body. Occasionally a cup was found, and this signified the tomb of a martyr, the cup having held his blood. The little chapel we were shown was destitute of adornment, and so small that it hardly seems possible that Christians could have met here for worship. It is a more probable hypothesis that this served as a funeral chapel.

From the Catacombs we drove to the Villa Albani, now owned by Prince Torlonia. This held at the beginning of the century one of the finest collections of Roman remains, but it was rifled of its gems by that arch fiend, Napoleon, and few were ever restored. A bronze statue of Apollo, a relief of Antinous, a wonderful thing, and another of the parting of Orpheus and Eurydice, were well worth seeing. The villa itself and its ruins were charming, and gave us an excellent idea of Roman country life. The Palazzo Doria was the next point of attack. Here we found many pictures of a high order of merit, for the most part portraits. It is not in many galleries that in one sweep of the eye one can take in a Rubens, a Titian, a Tintoretto, a Holbein and a Raphael. On the same wall also hung a Van Dyke, a Valasquez and a Piombo. Without exception we have found the best Velasquez, Piombo and Quentin Matsys which we have seen. In fact I never got at Matsys' power until I saw here The Money Changers.

So full a morning made me willing to stay in during the afternoon. The hours in doors can always be profitably devoted to reading and writing. Wednesday morning I was prepared for another tramp, and we started early for the Sculpture Gallery of the Vatican. Without exception this gallery ranks the highest of any we have seen or are likely to see. Its famous pieces are the Apollo Belvedere, the Laocoon, the Mercury, the Crouching Venus, the Torso of Hercules, and the Perseus of Canova. But these are by no means all its treasures. Many pieces of less note and more recently unearthed well repay study. I was again greatly struck with the fact that casts give no idea of the power of the marble. We went again to the Sistine Chapel, where we got an excellent light on Michael Angelo's stupendous work. The library was interesting, although at first sight it appeared like Hamlet with Hamlet left out, for no books were visible. Many gifts and relics were shown, among which were the very ugly baptismal font used in the baptism of the Prince Imperial of France, and some magnificent vases of Sevres china presented by different potentates. I had the great joy of beholding the precious Vatican manuscript of the Bible with my own eyes, but alas, it was not open to I. Tim. iii. 16!

The afternoon was quite as full as the morning. We took a carriage for a ride along the Appian Way as far as Porta Sebastiano, and under the Arch of Drusus, beneath which Paul passed in entering Rome. The tombs of the Scipios and the Columbaria lay on our route. Returning we stopped a little while to explore the Baths of Caracalla, a vast pile of ruins with few reminiscences of their ancient glories, save their vast size and some remnants of the mosaic pavement. Coming up to the Coliseum, we roamed for an hour about its vast and awful ruins. The Forum we spent some time in studying. Some way we have not yet got into the spirit of Rome. We see the spot where Cæsar lay in state, where Virginia was killed, where Curtius took his fatal leap, and yet neither is the blood stirred nor the brain fired.

ROME, Friday, 30 October.

In the morning we visited the Church of St. Giovanni in Laterano, and the Lateran Museum connected with it. This church is the Arch-Episcopal church, the mother and head of all the churches, ranking before St. Peter's. Here the Pope is crowned. The church itself was undergoing some repairs, and we did not see it so thoroughly as we should have liked. It is a fine basilica, but has been a good deal injured by injudicious alterations and decorations, and does not compare with St. Maria Maggiore in impressiveness. Two of the private side chapels, those of the Torlonia and Corsini families, were very beautiful. The former was an exquisite combination of white and gold.

The Baptistry gains interest from its great age and its reputed foundation by Constantine. Its architectural form has furnished the model for the greater number of the round baptistries in Italy. The museums are divided into Profano and Christiano, and were each interesting. We spent some time in deciphering inscriptions from the catacombs. The Museo Profano contains many exquisite remains of Roman art which have been unearthed in various places near Rome. Among them was a relief representing the funeral of a lady of rank.

In the afternoon I went to the Capuchin Church, and saw the picture of the Archangel by Guido, and visited that ghastly valley of dry bones, the cemetery. How a Christian mind could have conceived of anything so heathenish I do not know. We also visited some shops, where I squandered some of my patrimony. Friday morning Miss Randolph and I went out to look at photographs. In the afternoon I rode to St. Stefano Rotondo. Oh, the horrors of the pictured martyrdoms! I then went to the Palazzo Barberini, where I looked upon the haunting picture of Beatrici Cenci. Rome bristles with horrors. I love my own dear country. It is so free from the atrocities in which these lands are soaked.

Saturday morning we went to Palazzo Rospigliosi to see Guido's Aurora. Wonderful! Nowhere before have we seen painted such life and motion and such poetic motion. It is the onward dance which Byron describes, chasing the hours with flying feet. Next to the Sistine Madonna, and in a different way, it is the most attractive picture I have seen. St. Pietro in Montorio was our next objective point. A glorious view, frescoes said to be by Piombo from Michael Angelo's drawings, and a sight of the traditional spot of Peter's execution rewarded us. We stepped into St. Lorenzo in Lucina for the sight of a Guido's Crucifixion, hardly as fine as that at Bologna, and then I came home and Charles went to Barberini. In the afternoon we went to the engraving establishment and saw our engravings packed.

MILAN, 10 November.
PARIS, 15 November.

Rome is behind us and so far I do not regret it. I have felt so far from vigorous most of the time that sight seeing has been a burden. Nevertheless I dropped a penny into the fountain of Trevi, and I hope to come again with my daughter. We left Rome for Pisa at half past nine Monday morning. The journey to Pisa was through a

flat, uninteresting country, made interesting only by the
glimpses it gave of the Mediterranean and Elba.   The
city itself seemed not unlike Florence, situated as it is
on both banks of the Arno.   An early bed and an early
rise, in order that we might get the nine forty-five train
for Milan, was the programme.   The group of fine buildings which stand on the borders of the city, and include
the Duomo, the Campanile, the Leaning Tower, and the
Baptistry and Campo Santo, is perhaps the finest group
of buildings we have seen anywhere.   The Duomo,
Baptistry and Campanile at Florence hardly present so
striking an appearance.   The Baptistry is a marvel of
elegant designs and proportions.   Inside it is remarkable
for a fine specimen of the work of Nicholas Pisano.
The echo is something wonderful in its way, and as I
have never outgrown my childish liking for echoes, I
made the sacristan exhaust his vocal powers.   The inside
of the Cathedral presents a type of Italian Gothic, a
kind of union of the basilica with the Gothic which we
had not before seen. Here is the hanging lamp watched
by Galileo.

The Leaning Tower looks like all its pictures.   It is a
wonder.   We did not ascend.   The interior of the Campo
Santo is in appearance like the cloisters of a monastery,
but is a peculiarly delicate Gothic.   We drove hastily
back to the station through a pouring rain, and took the

train for Milan. The route to Genoa was charming. Most of the way it bordered the Mediterranean, often tunneling its way through rocks in order to make its passage. The glimpses of the sea through these rocks were charming.

At Genoa all we could do was to think of Christopher Columbus of blessed memory. We puzzled ourselves with the problem of where we should have been if that saint had never been born. It grew dark soon, and our ride through Lombardy to Milan had only the weariness of the final part of a long journey. At Milan we found our way by means of an omnibus to the Hotel Pozzo, a cheerless kind of a place with a shut-up smell, which made me anxious to make our stay in Milan as short as possible. This we did by working hard on Wednesday. Our first drive was to the banker's, where voluminous mail reached us, including very nice letters from Mary. We then drove to the Brera. This gallery is finely arranged and lighted, but, though a cold day, it was unwarmed. We therefore did not stay to examine the pictures in detail, but only the masterpieces. The pride of the Brera is Raphael's Marriage of the Virgin. The picture did not impress me, although it would be easy to catalogue its merits. A picture which interested me more was a study of the head of Christ, by Leonardo, for his Last Supper. I think that divinity shines in this face more strongly than any representation of Christ I have ever seen. The gallery introduced us to several new artists. Bernardino Luini is perhaps the best of them. Two fine Veroneses are also here. But the way in which we saw the gallery was unsatisfactory. Leaving it, we walked back through the beautiful arcade of Victor Emanuel to the Duomo—the wonderful Duomo. It is magnificently placed, and stands as a constant inspiration to holy thoughts and desires. But the truth must be told. It is dingy. The spires and dainty work, which must have looked like frost work when fresh from the artist's hands, show too clearly how long they have mingled with earth. The interior is grand, and caused us to exclaim again: ''The Gothic is the only architecture for a Christian church.'' Unfortunately the interior was much disfigured by the trumpery pictures and decorations, but the windows are glorious. Taking a carriage at the Piazzo Duomo we drove to the Church of Maria delle Grazie, in the refectory of whose monastery is all that remains of Leonardo Da Vinci's Last Supper. Here, as all over Europe, Napoleon's cloven hoof is seen. His soldiers, here quartered, amused themselves by disfiguring this magnificent work. It is defaced beyond all hope of restoration, but so long as one line is left its genius will survive. Some excellent copies were in the room. Going back to the banker's we found yet more mail, and we then rode to see some drawings of Leonardo and of Raphael. Those of the latter artist for his School of Athens, and some other frescoes were especially interesting. Walking back to the Duomo we stopped to engage our passage for Basle, and then went to buy photographs. We got back to the hotel for a late dinner and an early bed.

The early bed was the prelude to an early rise, for half-past five saw us on our feet, and at half past seven we were speeding toward Basle in a fine compartment car, of which we were the sole occupants. A journey so delightful as that of the 12th November, 1885, from Milan to Basle, by St. Gothard, I never experienced. Everything conspired to make it so, the finest of weather without and the most comfortable of cars within, and over the glorious Alps. We pierced mountains and we scaled mountains, we dashed over precipices and around precipices, and yet over more mountains higher and precipices more steep. Night did not settle upon us until, having passed Tell's home and Arth Goldau, we reached Lucerne. Even then the light was sufficient to show to us Hotel St. Gothard, which we had not expected to see again this year. At Basle we walked from the station to a near hotel, and found a comfortable resting place for the night. At quarter to nine we were on our way to Paris, on what I think was the fastest train I ever

traveled on for any length of time. We made hardly
six stops, and between six and seven o'clock were in
Paris. The country was flat and uninteresting. The
soil seemed poorer than I expected to find. The houses
were few, the population here as in other parts of the
continent being gathered into towns.

We went to a small hotel, Brittanique, for the night.
It was gloomy enough. The weather was as cold as at
home, and we were almost homesick in gay Paris. But
daylight put a brighter aspect on things. Our first care
was to look for permanent lodgings and to get our mail.
We decided on Hotel de la Tamise, a quiet little place on
Rue d'Alger, opposite the Tuileries Gardens. We have
a cozy room and are most centrally located. The first afternoon we spent in wandering about the wonderful streets.
The magnificence of this city is patent to the most super-
ficial observer. Its broad streets and boulevards, its
parks and squares, its palaces and magnificent public
buildings, combine to form a scene of unparalleled splendor. Our first Sunday in Paris passed much as all our
continental Sabbaths have passed. In the morning we
went to the American Church, of which Dr. A. F. Beard is
pastor. The edifice is really very pretty, and the congregation the largest and best looking, I think, we have seen.

Tuesday we began our work, systematic work, in
earnest. We spent the morning in the Louvre, going

through the sculpture galleries and making a beginning on the pictures. It is by far the best single gallery we have visited. In the afternoon we went to the Madeleine, a true Corinthian Greek temple. It is massive and impressive without, but it is not a church. The interior is gloomy, being lighted only from above. It is sombre and heavy, and has none of the litheness and spring which belong to a church. Over its doors, as over the doors of all the public buildings in this city, are those magic words, dear to the heart of the French Revolutionist, " *Liberté, equalité, fraternité.*" They seem used as a magic charm. We wandered about the streets and boulevards after the gas was lighted. The streets are brilliant and gay, crowded beyond compare. We came down the Rue Royale to the Place de la Concorde, and stood watching the tide of life, the innumerable lights, and the general brilliancy. It was a good place to stand to see the present. It was a good place to stand to reflect upon the past. It all seemed like a story of blood and rapine, of ungoverned passions and unholy vengeance. What iniquities have these streets not seen ! One realizes here the enormities which the history of France unfolds. Paris holds the larger part of them.

Wednesday morning found us again at the Louvre. The pictures are glorious. It is decidedly the most representative gallery we have seen. In it are found masterpieces of all the great masters. Its Murillos are the finest we have seen, and confirm my strong predilection for that artist. His Conception ranks, I believe, next to the Sistine Madonna. Indeed, in coloring and in the felicity of its conception, it is its superior. Murillo never puts in the lay figures of the saints, which so mar the ideal perfection of so many religious fancies. Titian is represented by many excellent works of a motif as different as the Entombment and Jupiter and Antigone. They all have deepened my judgment that Titian was incapable of so apprehending spiritual truth as to put it upon canvas. Two of the finest Correggios we have seen are those of Venus and the Satyr and the Marriage of St. Catharine. The only Leonardo of any interest to me, save his Last Supper, we find here. The Raphaels, though numerous, add very little to the impression he has already made upon me. I cannot regard him as always a pleasing artist. His contrasts are too violent. His Madonnas seem to me to have very little character. Rubens and Rubens' Wives are here. There is a coarseness about many of his figures which grows upon me after I have studied Italian art. His Triumph of Religion is a spirited piece, however.

In the afternoon we went over to the Island to visit the Notre Dame Cathedral. On the way we passed the beautiful Tower St. Jacques and the magnificent Hotel de Ville. The squares and public buildings are so grand. The church was not disappointing. Architecturally it is full of interest. Its rows of massive pillars and the exquisitely decorated chapels behind the choir made this church to us unique. But it was cold and dark, with few signs of worship. Churches do not seem to be frequented here by worshipers as in Italy. We walked round the Palais de Justice and the statue of Charlemagne and back to the hotel, after searching shops and shop windows for beautiful dolls for our daughter.

In the evening we went to one of the meetings of the McCall Mission. Lord Radstock spoke, and gave a clear, comprehensive gospel talk. I was pleased to find I could understand every word. It was quite novel to sing "Moody and Sankey" in French. But in French or English the old story is the same. We really seem to see more signs of evangelical earnestness than in any city since leaving London.

Thursday morning we visited the Pantheon. It is a massive building with a dome which seems to lift the whole pile upwards. The interior is in the form of a Greek cross and in the Corinthian style. The walls are decorated with scenes from the lives of the saints, but the art calls for no special mention. It seemed to me that the Revolutionists who set this building apart to the memory of great men interpreted the significance of its architecture more truly than those who consecrated it as a church. In the crypt, an extensive underground cavern, rests Victor Hugo. His tomb is covered with the memorials of friends, and wreaths are literally stacked in the church. In this crypt Voltaire and Rousseau lay until some persons in a fit of paltry vengeance flung their bodies out. The echo through these cavernous arches is the most remarkable I ever heard. It distinctly articulates words.

Friday morning we made a visit to the Place de la Bastille, the site of the old prison. There is nothing to remind one of the horrors of that horrid fortress. The situation is partly covered by shops, and in the centre of the Place a beautiful bronze column rises to commemorate the patriots who fell in the Revolution of 1830. These columns, which are erected in various places, are very handsome. That of the Place Vendome, in imitation of the Trajan column in Rome, is a magnificent affair of its kind. From the Bastille we rode around to the Madeleine through some of the finest boulevards, past the Portes St. Denis and St. Martin. The afternoon we devoted to an excursion to St. Denis. The ride was uninteresting, but the church would have repaid a much longer ride. This church has been for twelve hundred years the state church. Here the monarchs from Dagobert I. to Louis XVIII. have found a final resting place, and from the church their bones were taken and cast, by that hellish Revolutionary mob, into a common grave. By a strange revolution Louis XVI. and the unfortunate Marie Antoinette now repose in the despoiled vaults. The church is a very fine example of the transition from the Norman to the Gothic. Without but few marks of the Gothic are to be seen, but within the pointed arch is found in all its beauty. The stone of the interior is very pure, the windows, though of unfitting subjects, are rich and very numerous. The choir is raised, a novel feature.

Our evenings we spend in reading and planning our future work. I have been reading a short history of France, Hammerton's Round my House, and Dickens' Tale of Two Cities. I had forgotten how powerful a book this last is. Reading has almost made me fear to go to bed, and I find myself looking for Madame Defarge and her knitting.

Saturday morning we went to Père la Chaise. It did not appeal to us as a very beautiful city of the dead. We found the graves of Heloise and Abelard still strewed with fresh flowers. The French have a custom of highly decorating the graves of their friends with the most hideous wreaths of beads, dried flowers and tissue paper. The effect to our eyes is in execrable taste. Many of the distinguished dead of France lie here. The graves of Musset, of Thiers, of Périer we visited.

The afternoon took us to the Louvre to see the cabinet of drawings. Many of those by Raphael, Michael Angelo and Leonardo were of great interest. We lingered longest, however, in the rooms of the modern French art. Delaroche, Delacroix, Ary Scheffer and Ingres were the principal artists. In many ways the most striking picture we saw was one Victor Giraud, The Slave Dealer. It represented an eastern voluptuary surveying a shrinking Circassian. Two pictures of Delaroche, The Death of Queen Elizabeth, and The Sons of Edward IV. in Prison, were full of life and character. Scheffer's Temptation of Christ exaggerates all the defects of that artist. All of Ingres' were cold and dead. Troyon had two magnificent landscapes.

Sundays in Paris are a little more satisfactory than in some places. We seem to be within reach of decidedly Christian influences. In the afternoon we went to hear Père Hyacinthe. A magnificent sermon he preached. I was able to understand nearly every word, and was so borne away by the effort of listening and the excitement that I found myself quite exhausted. The subject was the separation in the future life between the good and the evil. He ranged himself on the side of Origen, and advanced the theory of punishment, of expiation, and final restoration. He used Scripture with great skill. His text was from

Peter, Christ preaching to the spirits in hell, but the passage he used with greatest power was from Revelation : " I am Alpha, etc., I hold the keys of death and of hell." Hell and its subjects are given to Christ. His apostrophe to Jesus was full of tender eloquence. The church itself seemed a kind of betwixt and between. Things were badly managed. One small boy seemed the chief functionary, and he attended to lighting the church and leading the choir, besides managing other affairs. The church building was small and bare, yet filled to its utmost capacity. The service began with the Lord's prayer and Apostles' creed, and resembled the English service, but was much shorter. The censer was swung and the holy water was at the door. Hyacinthe resembles Mr. Beecher very much. I have a suspicion that, like him, he may be a poor and unsafe leader. Certain it is, his movement is not growing as it was hoped.

PARIS, Monday, 23 November.

Our morning was spent in rather futile attempts to do a great many things we couldn't. We went to the Jardin des Plantes, where everything was closed, and then came up to the Palais de Justice. We tried to get into the Conciergerie, and found that a more difficult matter than in 1792. It was not open. But we wandered about the Palais de Justice to our hearts' content.

One hall is really very fine, the Salle des Pas-Perdus. The court rooms were numerous and small. The barristers who were to be seen promenading the halls in their robes and caps were a fine looking body of men. The remainder of the morning we spent in buying our daughter's doll. It, as everything in Paris, seemed dear, but none too dear for such a daughter. When we arrived home we found we had been honored by a call from Hon. R. M. McLane, Envoy Extraordinary, etc. One thing has surprised us in Paris. We find less courtesy here among all classes with whom we come in contact than in any other country. I find my French serves all purposes, although I feel I have a vantage ground when I can shop in *lingua vernacula.*

Tuesday morning was chilly. We took a ride in the Bois de Boulogne in the morning. The park is perfectly delightful, and was full of gay riders. One of the prettiest sights I ever saw was a mother having with her three golden-haired daughters on prancing steeds. The mother rode magnificently. In the afternoon we went to the Palais Luxembourg, but here we were balked, as it was closed for repairs. We spent a few hours pleasantly at the Jardin des Plantes. Things struck us as a little helter-skelter, and hardly well cared for. The Zoological Gardens do not compare with those of London or Berlin. The museum was of chief interest from an ethnological point of view. The collection included types of every known race of men. The conservatories were not specially interesting.

The days are so short here that it is really difficult to make a full day. Wednesday was quite rainy, and I only went out once. In the morning we went to the Louvre, and spent two hours among the bronzes, drawings, Egyptian and Greek antiquities and articles of *vertu*. The sight of the snuff boxes was enough to bring tears to the eyes, even though they had been long innocent of snuff. Some of the antiquities were wonderfully fine. Some of the drawings by the great artists were full of interest. The exuberance of Titian's fancy is seen in his drawings even more than in his paintings.

From the Louvre we went out, by the way the Empress escaped, to the church of St. Germain l'Auxerrois. It is a handsome Gothic church, but it is plain that the best life of the French has not gone into the churches, as in Italy. We next walked along the quay, and took an omnibus for the Gobelins tapestry works. We found these very interesting, both in the exhibition and in the manufactory. The process was much slower than I had supposed. Six square inches is a day's work. The velvet carpets here made by hand, though laboriously wrought, hardly seem to be superior in appearance to similar carpets of machine workmanship. It was three when we returned home, and thus our day's work out of doors was finished.

Thanksgiving Day.

Not very much like our customary day of Thanksgiving! In the first place the rain poured, an unusual occurrence, and in the next place we had neither turkey nor cranberry sauce. But we did go to church and listened for an hour while the good minister tried to prove (beginning with Adam) that we are living in the best days of the world. As if we had not realized that every day since we left home. From the church we took a carriage and rode to the Préfecture of Police, where we got permission to visit the Conciergerie. Few buildings are so full of melancholy interest. The narrow cell in which the unhappy Queen was confined still holds the chair in which she sat and the cross before which she prayed. It was not a dungeon dark and damp, but cold, cheerless and bare. By that irony of events which we so often see illustrated, the cell where Robespierre passed his last night adjoined that of Marie Antoinette, while just beyond was the room from which the Girondists went to the scaffold. It must have been with a sense of mighty triumph over her enemies that the unfortunate Queen passed from the cell through its low door to the scaffold. "Six francs for a coffin for the widow Capet." It was the last indignity that could be offered, and then she slept well. Oh, what a city of horrors is this !

Leaving the Conciergerie we drove to Napoleon's tomb. Here we saw the remnant of another drama. He sleeps, too. That brain, that heart, have long ceased to throb. The memorial is most fitting to that man who once convulsed Europe, and who rose to the summit of earthly grandeur and fell to the depths of earthly failure. In an open circular vault rests the sarcophagus of blood-red stone in which the body lies. Around it are figures of marble and battle flags fast falling to decay. The Church of the Invalides is hardly more than one vast tomb, for I think it doubtful if worship is ever here held. The architecture is Corinthian, and the marble of column and floor is white and fair.

The Hotel des Invalides itself, which we first visited, is an enormous building, but now sparsely inhabited. Around the court of honor run colonnades, similar to a cloister, and frescoed on these walls are scenes from the history of France. The Museum differs but little from other military museums. A pleasant and talkative soldier showed us several things of interest. Among them was a certificate of membership in the Society of Cincinnati given to a French General and signed by George Washington. The swords of Napoleon and the Generals, the saddles of the later Kings of France, including

Louis XVI. and Charles X., were of interest.   All these
things make me hate war more and more.   Would they
were all beaten into plow-shares and pruning hooks !

Friday proved to be the first bright day of the week,
and we were glad to improve it by going to Versailles.
We took the train at eleven thirty, from the Gare St.
Lazare, and in less than an hour were landed in the historic town. St. Cloud and Sèvres, through which we
went, should have had a visit. As it was, we
found our time insufficient for inspecting the unri-
valed attractions of the palace. The garden and park
we were obliged to pass without a look, except such as
we gained from the windows of the palace. I had not
supposed the buildings to be in a town, and it was therefore something of a surprise to drive up to the palace
gate through a no inconsiderable town. The exterior ap·
pearance of the palace does not differ materially from
similar buildings belonging to its period. It stretches
out a quarter of a mile in length, and incloses
numerous wings and courts. In the front court stands
a bronze statue of the Louis called the Great. We entered
the palace by the vestibule of the chapel, a beautiful
room of the early eighteenth century. The rooms of the
palace are now converted into picture and sculpture galleries, and a mere synopsis of the paintings would fill
this book. There were miles of them, and hardly a poor

picture among them. They represented every phase of
French history and every man great in the military or
political history of France, from Clovis to Napoleon III.'s
downfall. The battle scenes of Horace Vernet and the
diplomatic scenes of Gallait, the paintings of Ary Scheffer,
of David, of Gros, of Lebrun, of Gérard and Gérôme,
were true works of art. Days might be spent in those
rooms. The magnificence of the paintings almost ob-
scures the magnificence of the rooms themselves. The
Gallerie des Glaces is one of the most magnificently decorated rooms we have seen in Europe. The apartments
of the Queens, occupied by the three Maries, the wives
of Louis XIV., XV. and XVI., were elegant apartments.
But most touching were the cozy half-dozen little rooms
known as the petits apartments de Marie Antoinette.
Here were passed the happy days of that unfortunate
woman, and here her friends gathered as related by
Madam Campan. The bolts on the windows and doors
were made by the King, and bore her monogram. In
the room which contains David's magnificent paintings of
the Coronation of Napoleon and that of his Marriage to
Maria Louisa, stands also Vela's sculpture of the Last
Days of Napoleon, of which that at Washington is a re-
plica. We passed through last the Gallery of Battles.
Blood, blood, always blood ! Here we saw a painting of
The Siege of Yorktown, or, as it was spelled, Yorck-

Town, in which a French General is giving the orders
for a final charge, and George Washington stands in the
background.   Such are fame and fate !

We walked to the station, and at half past six were
eating dinner at Hotel de la Tamise.

Saturday again proved rainy, and going out proved
a duty rather than a pleasure.   In the morning we paid
our last visit to the Louvre, and spent most of our time
among the pictures.   Those of the earlier French school
we rather slighted upon our first visit, and to them we
gave a large share of attention.   I have very little reason to change the opinion of French art which I hitherto
formed.   Most of the pictures seem trivial, or cold or
sensational.   We were struck with one picture by
an   artist   before   unknown,   representing   the   scene
at the pool of Bethesda.   It was with a little throb
of regret that I turned my back on this great work.
The pictures we have seen have, on the whole, given me
great and lasting pleasure.

LONDON, Friday, 4 December.

Once more in the world's metropolis, for such this great,
smoky, dirty, muddy, foggy city is.   There is more to
it in every way than any city we have seen.   Paris, in spite
of its gay streets and glitter, did not seem to us prosperous.   The impression the place gave was one of living

beyond its means. And this the Government is certainly doing. The Republican ideas have taken deep hold on the imagination of the people, and I fear each is more desirous of obtaining liberty, equality and fraternity for himself than to give them to others. The rights of citizenship appeal to the Frenchman more than their duties. It is said a marked decline in the manners of the humble Parisians is discernible within the last few years. It must be so, if ever their reputation for courtesy was merited. Nowhere in Europe have we received less politeness from the common people. The cab conductors were hardly decently civil.

We left Paris with what we have not before had on the continent—a trunk. Our troubles began. It seemed doubtful if the hackman could manage it, modest as were its proportions compared with the conventional Saratoga. We had five francs and over to pay extra for its passage, and we spent some eight francs for it before we got it to our lodgings. The train was swift, and swayed so as to give us fore tastes of what the channel had in store. And what did the channel have in store? First, cruel separation! These channel boats are like a Quaker meeting house. Next, darkness and vile sickness. I had a very comfortable time. But when poor Charles staggered into the cabin after the boat was moored he looked as if he had never, never loved me. I had hard work to sustain him to the cars and get him covered with rugs. Our custom house examination was light. The box of blacking and homeopathic remedies alone excited the officer's suspicions.

Thursday rose as a typical London day, which is an intensified Boston day ; a sullen sky and persistent rain and slop. We took our dinner and went to the Doré Gallery, where for two hours we were intensely moved by the noble genius of that great artist. In some respects the most powerful modern picture we have seen is Christ on the way from the Judgment Hall to Calvary. The union of dignity, pity and of joyful sacrifice in the figure of the Saviour is wonderful. The Vale of Tears, Doré's last work, was to me very impressive. Representatives of every class of people from the King to the beggars are pressing to the cross-bearing Christ, who beckons from afar. In all some thirty pictures, besides sketches, are here exhibited.

Friday how it rained, and what a profitless day we spent ! I was the whole day in getting things ready to pack and in packing. We had intended to take a Canterbury pilgrimage, but were obliged to defer it until Saturday. We took a swift train at ten fifty-five, and returned at half past three, giving us three hours and a half in the quaint old town. We walked up to the Cathedral, and reached it through the Mercery Lane, the favorite resort of the pilgrims. It is a noble old Cathedral. Its tower is remarkable for its springy effect. The interior is divided quite entirely into two parts. The nave is of the fourteenth century, and is in no way remarkable. The choir, which is separated from it by a stone screen, is raised above the level of the floor of the nave, and is a most interesting example of the transition from the Norman to the Gothic. Its date is 1175. Several windows of the thirteenth century are of great beauty. Nothing is left of the shrine of Becket. Reformation zeal tore down the shrine and scattered the ashes, but the steps and flags worn by the feet and knees of the pious pilgrims who came to do homage at his tomb may still be seen. The place where he fell (not by the high altar) is likewise pointed out. The tomb of the Black Prince, overhung by the armor he wore at Crescy, makes the exploits of that brave prince seem very real. The crypts of the Cathedral are not only very interesting in themselves, but especially so from the fact they sheltered the Huguenots, who fled from France after the revocation of the Edict of Nantes. Here their looms were placed and here they met for worship. On the walls may be seen texts of Scripture not yet obliterated. A part of the crypt is still used for worship by some of the descendants of these men, who still retain their language.

A walk of a half hour brought us to St. Martin's, the oldest Christian church in England, the very cradle of our Anglo-Saxon Christianity. A small, quaint little church it is, beautifully situated on a quiet knoll overlooking the town, but it has been evidently much restored. We did not get into it, but peeped in through the locked gates. In the quiet little churchyard in front a lady was at work setting out plants.

Sunday we made a full day. In the morning we went to City Temple to hear Dr. Newth, but he did not preach. Yet we heard a most excellent sermon on repentance. In the afternoon we visited the Temple Sunday School in quest of ideas, but soon made up our minds that we could give these people more ideas than they could digest. One thing struck us, the teachers were very young, mere boys and girls. We next went down to Lincoln Inn Chapel, where we heard the service chanted by choir boys and priests, and also a sermon by Canon Wace.

Monday we tried to do a little work, and spent a part of the hours of daylight in the National Gallery and South Kensington Museum. It was pleasant to renew our impressions of these wonderful collections. Turner's greatness impressed itself anew. No other of the British school seems really great. At South Kensington we went through several rooms that we did not see before, and examined more carefully Raphael's cartoons. Christ giving the keys to Peter, although one of the most injured, seemed to me the finest. The face of our Saviour may be compared with that of the Transfiguration. Several modern pictures are of great interest. Napoleon watching the shores of France recede when on his way to St. Helena, is interesting from an historical as well as artistic point of view. Britannia's Realm was also striking. Several of Landseer's smaller pictures are here. The Forster manuscripts we found very interesting. They include several complete manuscripts of Dickens' novels, and letters from distinguished statesmen and men of letters, such as Napoleon, Charles I., Elizabeth, Milton, Wordsworth, Emerson, Longfellow, and others. Tuesday we finished up. I spent considerable time in Paternoster Row and in the Sunday School Union rooms, and made final purchases. Dr. Charles Dana Barrows lunched with us at the Holborn, where we sat long over the board. I stayed in during the afternoon, and at six o'clock dined with the Barrows, at the Grand Hotel, where we sat still longer over the board. Wednesday was consumed in packing. It was an Herculean task, and one we almost despaired of. We had intended to take the one o'clock train for Oxford ; instead we took the half past three. We bade London farewell with few regrets. At half past five we were in Oxford, and five minutes later we were shivering at the Randolph over a fire so insufficient as to make the cold more apparent. These English keep their houses mortally cold. In the evening we were talking with a Scotchman, and he spoke of 55° being the point at which they keep their rooms in winter.

NEW YORK, 20 December, 1885.

We landed from the Oregon in a biting wind, the anniversary of the Mayflower's landing. We had been lying off New York harbor since early morning, but it was noon before we disembarked. Edwin was on the wharf, and it seemed pleasant enough to see a familiar face.

THE END.